THE GOAT-FOOT GOD

'The mediaeval mind of the man returned from the dead knew no half-lights or compromise in the doctrines of sin and hell. According to all the standards of his world, he had sold his soul to the Devil and an eternity of hell-fire awaited him.

'She gazed back at him. The minutes were slipping away one after the other. A town clock chimed the hour. How much longer were they going to stay like this? She dared not move lest God knew what should be let loose upon her. She could conceive of Hugh Paston falling dead if the occupant of his body withdrew suddenly. Come what might, the first move must not come from her.

'Then the man, without taking his eyes off hers, slowly stretched out his hand and touched the back of hers with the tips of her fingers, as if feeling her pulse. The finger-tips were icy cold. It was indeed like the touch of the hand of the dead.'

DION FORTUNE

Perhaps no other occultist in the twentieth century has so fully combined a practical knowledge of magic with a thorough understanding of psychology as Dion Fortune. The first mass-market paperback editions of her famous novels are well overdue, marking as they do a peak of literary entertainment and a disturbingly authoritative introduction to the ancient teachings of the occult. The series includes:

THE DEMON LOVER

MOON MAGIC

THE SEA PRIESTESS

THE WINGED BULL

THE GOAT-FOOT GOD

The Goat-foot God

Dion Fortune

A STAR BOOK

published by

WYNDHAM PUBLICATIONS

A Star Book
Published in 1976
by Wyndham Publications Ltd.
A Howard & Wyndham Company
123 King Street, London W6 9JG

First published in Great Britain by
The Aquarian Press

Printed in Great Britain by
Richard Clay (The Chaucer Press), Ltd., Bungay, Suffolk

ISBN 0 352 39712 8

THE GOAT-FOOT GOD

Came the voice of Destiny,
Calling o'er the Ionian Sea,
'The Great God Pan is dead, is dead.
Humbled is the hornèd head;
Shut the door that hath no key –
Waste the vales of Arcady.'

Shackled by the Iron Age,
Lost the woodland heritage,
Heavy goes the heart of man,
Parted from the light-foot Pan;
Wearily he wears the chain
Till the Goat-god comes again.

Half a man and half a beast,
Pan is greatest, Pan is least.
Pan is all, and all is Pan;
Look for him in every-man;
Goat-hoof swift and shaggy thigh –
Follow him to Arcady.

He shall wake the living dead –
Cloven hoof and hornèd head,
Human heart and human brain,
Pan the goat-god comes again!
Half a beast and half a man –
Pan is all, and all is Pan.
    Come, O Goat-god, come again!

(From 'The Rite of Pan')

CHAPTER ONE

The double doors of 98 Pelham Street opened to the latch-key of their owner, who, to judge from his habiliments, had just returned from a funeral. The butler who advanced to meet him in the outer hall and take from him his neatly-rolled umbrella, his top-hat with the deep mourning band, and his close-fitting black overcoat, endeavoured to put into his expression the exactly right proportions of sympathy and deprecation.

Hugh Paston passed through the wide inner hall and into his study, shut the door behind him, and helped himself to a drink from the cocktail cabinet. He needed it.

He flung himself into an enormous arm-chair beside the hearth, and extended his feet to the electric fire. The soles of his shoes, wet with churchyard clay, began to steam, but he never heeded them.

He had just returned from the funeral of his wife, who had been killed in a motoring accident. The car had gone up in flames; and the proprietor of the Red Lion Hotel, at whose gates the accident had occurred, had identified the bodies as those of a Mr and Mrs Thompson, well known to him as frequent visitors for several years. However, an inscription inside the watch found on the man had identified him as Trevor Wilmott, one of Hugh Paston's most intimate friends, and an inscription inside the wedding-ring of the woman had identified her as Hugh Paston's wife.

What should be the attitude of a husband at once out-raged and bereaved? Should it be grief and forgiveness or a disgusted repudiation? Hugh Paston did not know. The thing had indisputably been going on for a considerable period; it must, in fact, have been going on from the earliest days of the marriage, if the inn-keeper's chronology were to be relied on. Had marriage with him been a disillusioning

7

experience for Frida? He sighed. So far as he knew, he had left nothing undone that he could have done. But evidently he had not filled the bill. He compared Trevor and Frida to Tristram and Iseult, and left it at that.

He rose suddenly to his feet. One thing he knew for certain, he couldn't stop in the house. He would go out for a walk, and when he was tired, turn in at some hotel and phone his man to bring along his things. He went hastily out into the hall, closed the big doors silently behind him and set out at a brisk pace northward. But by the time he had crossed Oxford Street, and was making his way through the modified version of Mayfair that lies beyond it, he had slackened his pace. He had had precious little food or sleep since the inquest and that is a thing which takes it out of a man.

Tired of going north, and finding that the district was beginning to get sordid, he turned sharp right, and in another moment found himself in a narrow and winding street of shabby aspect, given up chiefly to second-hand furniture-dealing and cheap eating-houses.

He sauntered on, dislodged from his contemplation of early Victorian mantel-piece ornaments and Oriental Brummagem by the reek of the eating-house next door, and paused in front of a second-hand bookshop across the front of which the words: 'T. Jelkes, Antiquarian Book-seller' showed faintly on the faded paint. The usual outside tables had been withdrawn owing to the heavy rain, but a kind of bin stood just inside the narrow entry that gave access to a half-glass door painted a faded green.

He began to pick over the contents of the bin idly. The assortment consisted chiefly of antiquated piousness and fly-blown fiction. A reasonably clean blue binding heaved up from the welter like a log in rapids, and he fished for it hopefully. It proved to be a battered library edition of a popular novel. He knew by the name on the binding that it would be readable, and the title intrigued him. 'The Prisoner in the Opal'—. It raised visions.

He soon found the paragraph that gave the book its title. 'The affair gave me quite a new vision of the world,' he read.

'I saw it as a vast opal inside which I stood. An opal luminously opaque, so that I was dimly aware of another world outside mine.' There was a curious fascination in the rhythm of the prose, and he read on, startled and absorbed by an account of the Black Mass celebrated by a renegade priest and a dissolute woman. Here was something that would certainly both hold the attention and intrigue the intellect.

He opened the dingy green door and entered, his discovery in his hand. The shop was in darkness, save for such light from the street-lamp as made its way between the volumes ranged in ranks in the window. The characteristic smell of ancient books was heavy on the air; but through that smell came faint wafts of another smell; aromatic, pungent, sweet. It was not incense; at least, it was not church incense; and it was not joss-sticks or pastilles. It contained something of all three, and something else beside, which he could not place. It was very faint, as if the draft of the opening door had disturbed vague wafts of it where they lay hidden in crevices among the books. Coming as it did immediately upon his reading of the Black Mass and its stinking incense, and coming in darkness, it affected him to a degree that startled him, and he felt with A. E. W. Mason's hero, as if 'the shell of the world might crack and some streak of light come through'.

He heard someone stirring in an inner room. Then a dim warm radiance shone across the floor in a broad streak, coming from under a curtain slung across a doorless gap between the books, and in another moment he saw the figure of a tall stooping man in a dressing-gown, or some such voluminous garment, thrusting aside the curtain and coming through into the front shop. The proprietor of the bookshop, if that were what he was, revealed himself as a great gaunt framework of a man, his loose clothes hanging slackly upon him. His ungirt dressing-gown with its trailing cords made him look like a huge bat hung up by its hooked wings in sleep.

Hugh held out towards him the grubby blue volume in his hand. 'I got this out of your cheap bin,' he said.

The bookseller peered at it. 'Now how did that get in

9

there?' he demanded, as if inquiring of the book itself. 'If it was in the bin, I'll charge you accordingly. But I wouldn't have exposed it to that indignity willingly. I have a regard for books.' He looked up suddenly and transfixed his interlocutor with a piercing glance. 'I have a feeling for them that some people have for horses. Shall I wrap it up for you?'

'No thanks, I'll take it as it is. By the way, have you got anything else in the same line?'

It was as if an iron shutter came down over the bookseller's face. 'You mean something else by A. E. W. Mason?'

'No, I mean something else about the – er – Black Mass.'

The bookseller eyed him suspiciously, not to be drawn. 'I have got Huysmans' *Là-Bas* in French. There are no books in English on the subject of the Black Mass, no books worth having, that is. I do not call sheer sensationalism a book. There is nothing, so far as I know, strictly on the subject of the Black Mass, but one or two interesting books on cognate subjects. *The Devil's Mistress*, for instance; and *The Corn King and the Spring Queen*. Perhaps you would like to look at them. I have got them here, if you would be so good as to step this way.' He drew back the tattered curtain that hung in the doorless gap between the bookcases, and Paston followed him.

He found himself in a smallish room, too lofty for its size. Such light as there was came from a green-shaded lamp that stood on a small table beside an ancient leather-covered arm-chair drawn up to the hearth. The lamp threw a small circle of gentle light on to the chair; the rest of the room was in a dim, warm gloom, for the fire in the old-fashioned grate was low.

Serge curtains were drawn carelessly across a long French window on the wall opposite the doorway by which they had entered, and beside them was a half-open door through which the corner of a sink was visible. Piles of dusty books filled the corners of the floor. A small kitchen table covered with a coarse blue and white checked table-cloth occupied the centre of the room, and was the only bit of furniture in the place that was not cumbered with books. The fire-place under its white marble mantel-piece was a beautiful bit of wrought-ironwork with high hobs at either side, on one of which a black earthenware tea-pot stood warming, and on the other a heavy, willow-pattern plate.

Upon the opposite side of the hearth to the arm-chair was a big, broken-springed, leather-covered sofa.

'If you will be so good as to take a seat—' the bookseller said. Hugh Paston sat down and found it much better than the chairs in his own house. He sank back into its roomy depths and relaxed. 'I am afraid I am keeping you from your supper,' he said.

'Not at all,' said the bookseller, 'I haven't begun to cook it yet. I have only made the tea. Might I – er – offer you a cup, if you would honour me? It seems a pity to let it stew and be wasted.'

Hugh Paston accepted, not wishing to hurt his feelings. Tea was not one of his beverages at the best of times.

The bookseller produced two large white cups with narrow gold lines round them and an odd little gold flower at the bottom of each. Hugh remembered having seen similar ones in the potting-shed of his boyhood's home. He believed they were used for measuring out weed-killer and insecticides. At any rate, no human being drank out of them. Into these roomy receptacles went some milk from a bottle. Soft sugar was shovelled in with what looked like a lead spoon, and then a stream of rich mahogany fluid was applied from the broken spout of the black tea-pot.

'This—' said the bookseller, handing him a cup, 'is a man's drink.'

It was hot. It was strong. And altogether it bore not the remotest likeness to tea as it was understood in his wife's drawing-room.

Hugh Paston had no means of knowing that shortly before his visit the vulturine bookseller had bought his usual evening paper, and had found an illustration in which the Press photographer had been lucky enough to catch one face clearly – the face of the chief mourner at a certain sensational funeral, and, staring at it, had murmured to himself: 'Poor devil!'

The old man had eyes of a very light bright blue, deep-set under superciliary ridges like a gorilla, and over-hung by eyebrows that would have served most folk for a moustache. He was clean-shaven, and his tanned leathery skin hung about his chops in folds, after the manner of a blood hound.

Hugh Paston, at first sight, had taken him to be somewhere in the eighties; but in actual fact he was a battered and dilapidated sixty-five, looking much older than he need on account of his dressing-gown, a garment usually associated with the infirm.

He, for his part, looking at the man opposite him, judged him to be in the early thirties, but that whatever might be his actual age, he would never look a young man again. He wondered whether he had been deeply in love with the woman who had died with her lover, and surmised that he had not. There was a hungry and restless look about his face that is not seen on the face of men who have loved, even if they have been crossed in love. This was a man, he thought, who was unfulfilled. Life had given him everything he wanted and nothing he needed. Lack of spiritual vitamins and a rachitic soul, was his diagnosis. He judged that there was too much idealism in this man to start him drinking, but that he would prove rash and erratic in all his doings unless a steadying hand were laid on him at the present juncture.

He was watching his visitor carefully, and observed that he was settling down and relaxing, and being not without experience in the ups and downs of life himself, knew that a reaction was on its way, and the fellow would soon feel more dead than alive. He wondered what could be done to tide him over his bad patch.

'I wonder if I might offer you some supper. It is getting late, and – I don't know about you but I am getting hungry.'

'Yes, now you mention it, so am I.'

The old man moved off through the door beside the French window, and Paston saw a little built-on kitchenette, small as a ship's galley. The pop of gas indicated a gas-stove behind the door, and in a few moments there was a noble sputtering.

The old man came in with a second plate and put it to warm beside the fire. The heavy black kettle was restored to the hob.

'Eggs and bacon suit you?' he inquired.

'Couldn't be better.'

In a surprisingly short space of time the bookseller re-appeared with a loaded tin tea-tray and began to shuffle a miscellaneous collection on to the table in the middle of the room. Hugh Paston thought he had never smelt anything so good in his life as that bacon, or seen anything that looked as attractive as the crisp edges of the fried eggs as the book-seller served them out of the frying-pan in which they had cooked.

They fell to. The old man did not seem disposed to talk, and Hugh Paston, who felt as if he had not had a meal for a week, did not feel disposed to either. They ate in silence. At the conclusion of the meal his host put the black tea-pot back in its place on the hob and filled it up from the kettle. Then he shuffled everything on to the tray with a terrific clatter and deposited his load in the kitchen. Then he re-turned to the now blazing fire and began to fill his pipe.

Hugh Paston was half asleep over his cigarette, his feet stretched out on the fireside stool and a cup of the well-stewed tea beside him. The events of the last painful days, even his married life with Frida, seemed to have slid into the remote backward and abyss of time. The old bookseller, looking at him, saw that he was more disposed to go to sleep than to do anything else. He rose, went to the window, drew back the curtain and peered out into the darkness. Nothing was to be seen. Rain ran in long streaks down the glass. A furious draught drove through the cracks and swayed the tassel on the cord of an undrawn blind.

'A beast of a night,' he said, dropping the curtain back into place and returning to the fire.

Hugh Paston roused himself wearily. 'What time is it?'

'Getting on for late. Have you far to go?'

Hugh named a hotel he knew.

'Good Lord, what are you doing there?'

'God only knows. I couldn't stand the house so I cleared

out.' It never occurred to him that he had told the bookseller neither his name nor history, yet he took it for granted that the old man knew all about him, as in fact he did.

The bookseller looked at him thoughtfully.

'You can't go back there. Look here, can I offer you a bed for the night? You're very welcome.'

'That's very kind of you. Yes, I'd be glad to accept.'

The old man took the lamp in his hand and led the way into the shop. In one corner was a narrow wooden stair. They mounted two dusty flights of rickety stairs and his host opened a door next to the bath-room. 'Here you are,' he said. 'No bugs. I guarantee that. That's all I can guarantee, though.'

Left alone, Hugh Paston took stock of his quarters. The bed was not exactly a four-poster, but had two high poles behind, from which a canopy stuck out. Curtains of faded red damask hung from it after the unhygienic fashion of an earlier age. Hugh got out of his clothes and slid into the bed, which consisted of a huge, fat old feather mattress, half a dozen washed-out blankets, and a faded patchwork quilt.

When he awoke it was broad daylight, and his host, still in the same old dressing-gown, but with pyjamas under it, stood looking down at him with an immense mug in his hand.

'Here's some tea for you. Get up when you feel like it. There's no hurry.' He waved his hand and departed.

Breakfast was one of the most agreeable meals, thought Hugh, that he had ever eaten. The tea-pot stood on the hob and kept really hot, and they made toast on their forks in front of the glowing coals. It only needed a dressing-gown like the old bookseller's, and a pair of carpet-slippers, to be perfection.

'Why are you doing all this for me?'

The old man wagged his tufted brows at him. 'God only knows!' he said.

Paston laughed. 'You've heard my story, I take it?'

'I know what's in the papers, and guess the rest.'

'There's no rest. The papers got the lot.'

The old man did not answer.

'Well, I'm damned grateful to you, anyway. God knows what I'd have done to myself if I'd had to spend the night alone in that hotel.'

The bookseller rose. 'I've got work to do,' he said. 'Make yourself at home. There's plenty to read. Don't let the fire out.' He disappeared through the curtain into the shop.

Left to his own devices, Hugh Paston put his feet up on the sofa and settled down to his cigarette. Among the grubby cushions lay the book that he had bought the previous evening. He fished it out and commenced to flick over its pages.

Presently the old bookseller finished his chores and returned to the room behind the shop. Once the mail orders had been dealt with, there was apparently nothing to do for the rest of the day but sit around and wait for casual customers to drop in, and as the weather was worse than bad, it was improbable that they would.

At about lunchtime there came a great pounding at the door.

'That's Mrs Hull,' said the bookseller, and went to admit the char, who came barging in like a ship in full sail, hung about with purchases, mostly wrapped in newspaper. The old bookseller gave her some loose silver from his trouser pocket, without troubling to count it, and she barged out again.

He flung the now bulging black oilcloth bag on the table, where it disgorged everything imaginable.

'Absolutely trustworthy,' he said, 'and a great comfort to me. That's the right sort of woman to have about the place. Gets on with her job and clears off when finished.'

The bookseller began to get on with the preparations for a meal. There was a pound of pale pink pork sausages, showing through their damp bit of greaseproof paper, and a large dollop of mashed potatoes in a basin, evidently fetched from the neighbouring eating-house and only needing warming. Hugh Paston leant against the jamb of the door leading to the kitchenette and watched the old boy at his cooking. The frying-pan presented quite an attractive sight as the pale pink sausages gradually browned.

The old bookseller turned them out of the frying-pan, and

picking up the white china basin containing the mashed potato, held it out at arm's length and smacked its bottom, dodging skilfully back as the hot fat splashed out of the pan as the potatoes sploshed into it. Hugh Paston, cigarette between his teeth, was shaken with internal mirth. He thought of his butler. He thought of his chef. He thought of the head-waiters of fashionable restaurants. He wondered what his friends would make of him.

He suddenly realized that he was more intimate with the old bookseller than he had ever been with anybody in his life. He had a feeling that the light-blue eyes under their thatch of whiskers saw far more deeply into his soul than he was capable of doing himself.

His meditations were interrupted by having the large black tin tea-tray thrust into his hands. The old man loaded the dinner on to it, and Hugh Paston lugged the heavy load into the living-room. Without waiting to be told, he filled up the big black kettle and set it on the hob, ready for the everlasting tea. He reckoned that the old bookseller, with his tea-pot and his frying-pan, his broken-springed sofa and his cock-eyed feather-bed, had saved his mental balance and seen him safely through his time of crisis. How it had been done he had no means of knowing.

The old bookseller ate fast and the meal concluded with a slab of moist sultana cake and tea. Paston was hoping to get down to a good chin-wag, when the old bookseller suddenly put two grubby books into his hands and said:

'Amuse yourself with these. I always have a snooze now,' and suiting the action to the words, he settled himself back in his chair, opened his mouth, and went to sleep forthwith. Hugh Paston, who could not drop off to sleep like that, settled down to look at the books that had been given him.

They were the ones that the bookseller had previously recommended: *The Devil's Mistress*, by Brodie Innes, who was a 'writer to the Signet', whatever that might be, and *The Corn King and the Spring Queen*, by Naomi Mitchison, a tale of ancient Sparta.

He dipped into her first, and read the opening chapter upon the magic of the Scythian witch. He had learnt something of native magic during his safari expeditions, and knew the tremendous power of auto-suggestion upon the primitive mind. It was odd, very odd, to find the same kind of witchcraft in modern Africa and ancient Scythia. He settled down to read steadily the account of the rites of the spring ploughing. The dingy, cosy room disappeared from before his eyes as he saw in his imagination the woman lying nude in the centre of the great field, gazing up at the little white clouds of spring in the sky above her, and feeling the cold wind and the spring sun on her bare skin while the slow-moving, snow-white oxen dragged the primitive plough nearer and nearer as they circled the field.

He read on; but the fate of the royal house of Sparta interested him less, and he put the book down and took up the other.

Here was a tale of an entirely different calibre, based on the account of the witch-burnings in the state papers of Scotland. The old spell: 'Horse, hattock, to horse and away!' delighted him. It had the authentic ring. He chuckled at the picture of the handsome, vigorous Isabel Goudie putting the broomstick to bed with her stupid and boring husband and slipping off to the witch-coven in the old churchyard to enjoy herself with the Devil. He wondered what it was that made decent, sober Scottish matrons and maids kick up their heels and get their legs over the traces like this. He could understand their resorting to the rural Scottish equivalent of a night on the tiles, but why this adoration of the Devil? Why the religious element in it all?

He chuckled to himself at the idea of some respectable burgher playing the part of the Devil, complete with cow's horns, two on his head and one in his hand. He chuckled so loudly that he woke the old bookseller. 'Humph,' said Jelkes, 'You stick to sausages.'

But while nominally snoozing, the old man had been doing a lot of thinking. He had brought Hugh Paston to shore in the thick of the storm, it was not in him to stand idly by and watch him slip back into deep water again. Yet what could he do with the fellow? To invite him to prolong his visit, would, he felt, be an error of tactics. Paston belonged to a different world. He might be well enough content to picnic for a night or two on an old feather-bed but he would not care to keep it up for long. No, Hugh Paston must be returned whence he came on Monday.

But what would happen to him then? There was something fundamentally wrong with the fellow. It was much more, and it dated back far earlier, than the wife's defection. He wondered what inner emotional history lay behind Hugh Paston. There were powerful undercurrents that were making the surface so choppy, and their owner was the last man to know what they were.

They made tea. Hugh Paston tried to count up the number of cups they had already drunk between them that day, but failed hopelessly. The storm had returned and was sheeting down the window, which was tight shut against it; and his cigarettes and Jelkes' pipe and the blazing fire all united to produce a most comfortable frowst in which the soul was set free to range the heights of fancy while the body sprawled, too enervated for movement.

'Well?' said the old bookseller. 'So you've read the books, have you? And what do you make of them?'

'Don't tell me that they worked the Black Mass in Calvinistic Scotland. They wouldn't know how.'

'No, precisely. Huysmans brings that out clearly. You have to have a pucka priest for the job.'

'But you can get the book of the words anywhere. It's all in the prayer-book.'

'There's a lot more in it than the words. Do you know that it takes a priest a year after he's ordained to learn to say Mass? I know what I'm talking about. I nearly became a priest after being educated by the Jesuits.'

'What did you boggle at? Couldn't you manage the faith?'

'I could manage the faith all right. What I couldn't manage was the humility.'

Paston looked at the craggy old vulture, and believed him. 'Could you work the Black Mass if you wanted to?'

'If I wanted to, yes, I know enough for that. But I don't want to.'

'Then you have been actually ordained?'

'No, I never got as far as that. But one couldn't be on the inside of things, as I was in the seminary, without picking up a good deal if you had your eyes open. I saw a lot then which I learned to understand later.'

'What do you think of the Jesuits, if it isn't a tactless question?'

'I think they are the most marvellously trained body of men in the world – and the most dangerous if you get on the wrong side of them. I think they make certain fundamental mistakes, but I admire them. They taught me a lot about the power of the trained mind.'

'Is that what makes the difference when a priest says Mass?'

'Yes, that, and the tremendous momentum of the Church itself backing him up. That is why the Roman Catholic Mass has a kick in it that the Anglo-Catholic hasn't. The C. of E. doesn't know how to train her men.'

'Then it isn't just a matter of theology?'

'No, it's a matter of psychology – in my opinion, at any rate, though that's rank heresy, according to all the authorities.'

'Look here, Jelkes, will you work the Black Mass for me, for a lark?'

'No, you bloody fool, I won't, it's much too dangerous.'

'But you've just said it's only psychology.'

'Maybe, but have you thought what you'd stir up in yourself?'

'There's nothing I know of that I hold sacred. Huysmans' kind of Black Mass wouldn't have any kick in it for me. But look here, T. Jelkes, you come clean. You keep on dangling the carrot in front of the donkey's nose, and I keep on hee-hawing at it, but as fast as I try to close with it, you move it away.'

'Well, what is it you want?'

'Oh, damn it all, I don't know! But I want something, that's quite certain.'

'Do you "yearn beyond the sky-line where the strange roads go down"?'

19

'No,' said Paston, suddenly thoughtful, 'and that's my trouble, I believe. There aren't any roads in my life, not even strange ones. It would be better for me to have devil-worship than nothing.'

Jelkes grinned his camel-grin. 'We may be able to manage something a bit better for you than devil-worship,' he said.

'Who's we?' asked Paston quickly.

The bookseller brushed him aside with a wave of his hand. 'You still haven't told me what it is about these books that attracts you.'

'The smell of sulphur, I think, if you want the sober truth.'

'Well, there are times when civilized men – and women too, for that matter, need sulphur, just the same as horses need salt. It is that need that sent the Bacchantes out to dance with Dionysus on the mountains and tear fawns to bits.'

'Ever read *The Bacchae*, T.J.?'

'Yes. Euripides knew that man cannot live by bread alone. He wants a pinch of sulphur occasionally.'

'It might have been all right for the Greeks, but if I go up to happy Hampstead, and take off my togs and tear a leg of mutton to bits, there'll be trouble with the police.'

'Yes,' said the old bookseller sadly, staring thoughtfully into the fire, 'I'm afraid there will. The Black Mass is a sort of break-away from convention. It is a reaction, my son, a reaction to an overdose of the true Mass.'

'Can one have an overdose of that?'

'One can have an overdose of anything that is strong enough to be medicinal. You take too much health salts and see how you feel.'

'T.J., you're an awful old pagan.'

'I'm a comfortable old pagan, my lad, and I thank God for it.'

'Well, I'm a pagan, T.J., but I'm not comfortable.'

'When were you happy last, Hugh?'

'It's odd you should ask me that question, because it's one I've been asking myself. Do you know, I can hardly remember. I've had precious little happiness in my life, and yet I suppose I've had everything a fellow could want. I've always seemed to be sort of making the best of things and enduring them as philosophically as I could.'

'Was your marriage happy till it cracked up?'

'Yes, it was. Frida was the perfect wife. I had no fault to find with her until the inquest.'

'And yet you don't impress me as having been particularly fond of her.'

'Well, I was and I wasn't. I was loyal to her, and we got on all right. We never had a wrong word. She'd always seemed perfectly contented. And yet the marriage could not have satisfied her or she wouldn't have stepped outside, would she?'

'Was she forced into the marriage against her inclinations, or did you get her on the rebound from someone else?'

Hugh Paston sat staring into the fire, his cigarette extinct between his lips. At last he removed it and said: 'Do you know who it was introduced me to Frida, and practically made the marriage – it was her cousin Trevor Wilmott, the fellow she subsequently carried on with.'

Jelkes raised his massive eyebrows.

'Was it now? So that was the game!'

'I don't know. It never struck me there was a game. Trevor was my great pal at college, and when we came down, we were both rather at a loose end; he couldn't get a job, and I had nothing to do but chew a silver spoon.'

'And then what happened?'

'You think I was married for my money, then.'

'Looks like it to me.'

Silence fell in the dingy room, darkening to twilight. The fire was low, but the old bookseller did not stir to put coal on.

Finally Paston broke the silence. 'But why did Trevor go out of his way to make that marriage?'

'Did you ever read a book by Henry James called *The Wings of a Dove*?'

'No, what's it about?'

'A man and a woman love each other, but they can't afford to marry. They arrange between them that the man shall marry a rich woman who's dying of consumption.'

Hugh Paston sat silent for a while. 'Yes, I suppose that's it,' he said at length. 'I suppose I was the milch-cow that financed the liaison. God, what a world! I think I'll go out for a walk.'

'It's raining cats and dogs.'

'Doesn't matter. I want some air.'

CHAPTER TWO

At first Hugh Paston walked aimlessly about the dark streets, thankful for the cool, damp, rain-washed air after the stuffy heat of the room behind the shop. The revelation to which the old bookseller had led him had certainly been a tremendous shock. He knew that the old man had effectually lanced the abscess on his soul and it now ought to have a chance to heal. All the same, he harboured no delusion that he was out of the wood. He did not like the feel of himself. He still felt unnatural. He wondered whether the old bookseller had come on the scene too late to give him any real help. If he had known it, the old man whom he had left in the stuffy room behind the shop was wondering exactly the same thing, and was more than a little worried at the result of his playing with souls. It is one thing to have grasped the theory of psychoanalysis, but quite another to apply it in practice.

In a little while Hugh Paston ceased his aimless wandering and set out resolutely towards his house. It was no great distance, and his long legs carried him over the ground rapidly in the empty streets.

Arrived there, he admitted himself with his latch-key into the darkened hall. At the end of the hall was a swing-door, and passing through this, he found himself on the back-stairs. Going down a short flight, he came to a door on the half landing under which showed a line of light. He knocked, and a woman's voice with a slight Scotch accent bade him come in.

He entered a small room, much too full of knick-knacks, and a short square-set woman with greying hair rose to greet him. 'Good evening, Mr Paston.'

He said, 'Sit down, Mrs Macintosh', and she did so, still silently, looking at him questioningly.

'Mrs Macintosh,' he said, 'I am going to give up this

house.' She nodded, expressing no surprise. 'I want you to pay off the servants. Give 'em all three months' wages. It's no fault of theirs the place is closing down. Take everything out of my bedroom and stick it into trunks – all my personal things, I mean, I don't want any of the furniture; and take all my papers out of my desk and put them into deed-boxes, and put the lot into store. Then put the house in the hands of the agents and get them to hold an auction of everything, lock, stock, and barrel.'

'What about – Mrs Paston's things?'

Hugh Paston's face twitched.

'Sell them too.'

'But what about her papers, Mr Paston?'

Hugh sat silent for a long time, the woman watching him with pitying eyes.

Finally he spoke. 'Yes, those have got to be dealt with, but I can't do it now. Can't be done. Look here, you put them all into deed-boxes and store them along with the rest of the goods, but keep them separate from my papers, you understand?'

'Very good, Mr Paston,' said the housekeeper quietly, 'you can rely on me.'

'Thanks, yes, I know I can,' he said, and rising abruptly to his feet, he wrung her hand and was out of the front door before she had finished rubbing her tingling fingers.

Although it was after closing-time when he got back to Billings Street, he found the shop lit up, and the half-glass door yielded to his pressure. At the first ting of the bell the old bookseller was through the serge curtain, for the more he thought about the way his guest had taken things, the more anxious he had become.

Hugh Paston followed him into the room behind the shop, flung his hat on the table, and dropped into his old seat on the sofa. His action reassured the old man, for he could see he felt at home.

'Well,' he said, 'I've done the deed.'

'What deed?' cried Jelkes aghast, wondering if it were a murder.

'Given orders for the servants to be paid off and the house

24

sold up. Got rid of everything except my duds. Oh yes, and my wife's papers. Those have got to be tackled sometime, but not now.'

The old man heaved a sigh of relief. 'Well,' he said, 'I guessed you've earned your supper.'

'Yes,' said Hugh Paston, 'I guess I have.'

The frying-pan and tea-pot came into action, and the amicable, silent meal was partaken of and cleared away. But although relieved concerning his immediate anxiety, for his guest had neither blown his own nor anyone else's brains out, the old bookseller did not like the look of him at all. The hopelessness and apathy had given place to a kind of repressed excitement that struck the old man as being far from wholesome, and as likely to lead to rash acts, the consequences of which might have to be paid for heavily.

It was not easy for Jelkes to understand the viewpoint of this man sitting silently smoking on his broken-down sofa. He was of a different class and traditions; of a different generation, and a totally different temperament. Jelkes' mother had been left a widow in reduced circumstances, and though not a Catholic, had solved the problem of his education by sending him to the cheap but excellent school in the neighbourhood run by some Jesuit fathers. She was assured that no attempt would be made to convert the boy, and was satisfied with the assurance. No attempt had been made, but among the teachers was, as always, a man of marked charm of character, and to him the lad became deeply attached. No attempt needed to be made to convert that boy, he came knocking at the door of the fold of his own accord. And not only did he enter the fold, he aspired to the priesthood. He felt he had a vocation; and the very experienced men who judge of such things also thought he had a vocation. But he had been caught too late. A robust and rugged character had begun to be formed before he reached the seminary. The sports field of his preparatory school had done its work. He could not fit in with the whispering and influencing and routine humiliations. He bowed his neck to the yoke in the first flush of his faith; but presently he asked to be released. His friend came and pleaded with him. And not only pleaded with him, but wept over him, wringing his hands in despair. The whole experience made a terrible and searing impression on the adolescent lad. He had not taken the actual vows, being still in his novitiate, but the strongest admonitions of chastity had been impressed upon him, and these, together with his friend's heartbroken revelations of feeling, had prevented him from ever looking upon a woman to love her. A priest at heart, he had passed through life in complete spiritual isolation; a mystic by temperament, he was denied all spiritual consolation by his critical brain.

Penniless, without any qualifications, he by great good fortune got a job as assistant to a second-hand bookseller, found the trade congenial, and developed an aptitude for it, for he was a lad of well above the average capacity, as his teachers at the seminary had seen. Spending nothing on girl friends, or making himself attractive to the feminine eye, he saved steadily, and by the time he was forty, had launched out into a shop of his own. He soon prospered sufficiently to satisfy his simple needs, and these being satisfied, declined to exert himself any further, but enjoyed life after his own fashion, which consisted in a pot of tea on the hob, his toes on the fender, a book in his hand, and the collecting of the queer literature that interested him.

He had come across a translation of Iamblichos' curious work on the Egyptian Mysteries; this, coming on top of what he already knew of the Method of St Ignatius, gave him a revelation that was little less than a second conversion, for he saw here in a sudden flash that he had glimpsed the key to the technique of the higher consciousness. This served to start him off again on the ancient Quest – the quest of the light that never shone on land or sea. He had suddenly won to the knowledge that there was another kind of mysticism in the world beside the Christian mysticism. Ever since then he had pursued strange byways of thought, following up every bold speculation in science, every new viewpoint in philosophy.

The Search for the Absolute took hold of the untidy scholar among his dusty books, and kept him serene and happy as the years slipped by and brought him neither fame nor fortune but only the merest pittance, for he did not choose to exert himself.

He had had a good grounding in scholarship among the Jesuits and was familiar with the classical languages and had a working knowledge of Hebrew. Consequently he was able to go to the fountain-head of most things except Sanskrit. But however much he might find his own satisfaction in playing chess with the Absolute, he realized it would be little use to offer this kind of bread of life to Hugh Paston in his present state; or for the matter of that, in any state. Paston was a man who had been starved of life; who had starved in the midst of plenty without realizing what was the matter with him.

He was relieved to find that his guest, having disposed of his more pressing affairs, seemed quite content to enjoy the homely concoctions of the frying-pan and amuse himself by browsing on the shelves. He watched him browse, knowing that here he would find the surest key to the man's character, and noted with interest the old armful he brought over to the sofa and settled down with. He had got the treasured Iamblichos, he noticed; and an odd volume of Mme Blavatsky; and, of all incongruities, another book of Huysmans' *A Rebours*. Jelkes watched him go from one to the other, and back again. *A Rebours* he reckoned Paston had picked up because of his interest in Huysmans' other book, and was surprised to see him settle down to read it. Time went by; the old bookseller started a fresh brew of tea that was to form a night-cap, and put a cup by his guest's elbow unnoticed.

Hugh Paston looked up suddenly. 'I've found my Bible, Jelkes,' he said.

'Good God,' said the old bookseller, 'I like your taste in Bibles! If you were my son, you'd go face downwards across my knee. You're not a child, Hugh Paston – surely you have a more mature taste in literature than that!'

'Come, come, now, you wouldn't call *A Rebours* a kids' book, would you?'

'I'd call it a pimply adolescent's book. Anybody who'd cut his wisdom-teeth ought to be sick over it.'

'But can you imagine a mixture of *Là-Bas*, and *A Rebours*, with a dash of Iamblichos and Ignatius?'

'I can, but I'd sooner not.'

'It's not as bad as it sounds. Let me put it this way. I've got to equip some sort of a place to live in. I'm going to do it *à la* Huysmans, not because I'm really a degenerate, like his blessed Des Esseintes, but because it amuses me and gives me something to do and to think about. Now supposing I furnish my place *à la* Iamblichos; that is to say, I build up a 'composition of place' with a view to getting in touch with the old pagan gods, and then express it in furnishings? Supposing I live in the middle of those furnishings, day in and day out, and supposing I put my imagination behind it all, as it were, like a priest saying Mass – won't I get some sort of a Real Presence – of a pagan kind?'

'My God, Hugh, do you realize what you're talking about?'

'Yes, I do, but you don't. You think I'm talking about the Black Mass. But I'm not. I'm simply saying that there's more than one sort of contact with the Unseen.'

'I'd be glad if you wouldn't say it in my hearing.'

'T.J., I believe you're scared! Do you expect me to raise the Devil on the spot?'

'Laddie, I know a lot more about these things than you do. I *am* scared, and I don't mind admitting it. Now tell me seriously, do you really believe that these antics you propose performing will yield any genuine results, or are you just playing at them?'

'T.J., I don't know, and I want to find out. I can tell you one thing, however, if there is no invisible reality, and everything is just the surfaces I've always thought it was, I shall blow my brains out and go peacefully into oblivion, for I just can't stand it, and that's the sober truth, and I'm not joking.'

'I think I'd better make some fresh tea,' said Jelkes. He pottered about in the kitchenette, boiling up a kettle from cold on the gas-ring instead of using old black Sukie sitting on the hob, as was his usual economical habit.

It certainly needed some thinking out. He could see

exactly what Paston was driving at. He proposed to imitate Huysmans' decadent hero by making every object that surrounded him minister to his moods and have a definite psychological value. His aim, however, was not to produce aesthetic sensibility, but to get into touch with those old, forgotten forces hinted at in the various books. Hugh Paston, he saw, believed them to be objective, and Jelkes did not think it wise at the present juncture to disillusion him; he himself, however, knew from his thirty years' strange reading and experimenting, that they were subjective, and God only knew what hells and heavens a man might open up in his own nature by such means as Paston proposed to use.

But he certainly could not open any hell that was not already there; and if there were a hell there, according to Freud it was best to let the devils out for an airing occasionally. But even so, the old man was aghast at the possibilities that opened up. But it was too late to stop it now. Hugh Paston had got the bit between his teeth, was impatient of all control, and would go on from sheer bravado.

It seemed to him that the best thing he could do would be to throw himself into Paston's plans, and lay at his disposal the vast stores of odd knowledge that he had acquired, but never used, in the course of a lifetime's reading. Hugh would be exceedingly busy for months to come collecting his impedimenta from the ends of the earth; that would give him something to occupy his mind, and by the time the house was equipped, he might have returned to normal. Jelkes bore the tea-pot triumphantly into the sitting-room, having arrived at this solution.

Hugh Paston, with a very flushed face, was busy turning over the pile of books that lay beside him on the sofa. 'T.J.,' he exclaimed as the old man entered, 'I'm on the trail of something. I don't know what it is, but I can feel it in my bones.'

Jelkes grunted and slammed down the tea-pot. 'You're on the trail of a hell of a lot of trouble if you don't watch out. Now look here, Hugh, there is a way of doing what you want to do, a way of doing it properly, not in this hit or miss fashion you've got in your mind, and I'll show you what it is, provided you'll handle it the way I say, and not let us both in for a pickle.'

'I thought there was, you old devil, and that if I burnt enough sulphur under your nose, you'd come clean. Now where do we start?'

'You start with that cup of tea.'

'Right. Now I'll tell you what's in my mind, and we'll see if we both have the same idea. I think we ought to start by invoking the Great God Pan.'

The old bookseller groaned inwardly, shades of the seminary gathering about him. He did not repudiate the idea however.

'How do you propose to make a start?' he inquired mildly.

'I propose to get hold of a suitable house, one of those big, left-over country mansions with lots of huge rooms, that are white elephants to everybody, and fit up the different rooms as temples to the different gods of the old pantheons. Make a really artistic job of it, you know. Have some first-class frescoes done, and all the rest of it; and I'm inclined to think that if we make the temple ready, the god will indwell it, and we shall begin to learn something about him – or her.'

The old bookseller groaned again.

'Now, T.J., I'll provide the wherewithal – it's about the only thing I can provide, God help me – if you'll provide the ideas, and then we want someone to do the designing and chase about after the oddments. I know various firms who go in for designing houses from the attic to the cellar in any period or a mixture of 'em all, but I don't know of anyone who could do this job, do you? I expect we'll have to wrestle with it ourselves, and get hold of a tame artist who'll do as he's told.'

'That sort isn't usually much of an artist,' said T. Jelkes.

'Well, can we get hold of an artist who's along this line of thought?'

That was the exact crux of the matter, and that was what T. Jelkes had touched upon and discarded while he was brewing the tea. Paston had put his finger upon the spot; they must have their master-craftsman for the making of any temple of the Mysteries. There was another thing Hugh Paston must have, only he didn't know it, he must have his priestess. Two men couldn't work the thing between them. And God only knew where the thing would end if they introduced a woman into it. He knew where it usually ended in pagan times.

And he had the priestess ready to hand if he chose to lay his hand on her. But did he choose? No, he did not. Paston could go to hell before he'd do that. But on the other hand, the work would be a godsend to the girl, who needed it badly. He was very anxious about her. Things had not been going well with her lately. Two of the papers she worked for had closed down, owing her money. He suspected she was not getting anything like enough to eat. Would it be possible to get her the job of doing all the craftwork and designing, which was her trade, and yet keep Hugh Paston from playing the fool with her?

He considered his guest critically. He did not think he would be a man especially attractive to women. He was tallish, loosely built, and carried himself badly, with awkward, jerky, nervous movements. He had the long-fingered, bony hands of a psychic and sensitive, and Jelkes guessed that the rest of his physique was to match. His strength, he guessed, would not be muscular, but would depend upon nervous energy; and he judged by the jerky, awkward movements that at the present moment everything was disco-ordinated, and the fellow had no stamina or staying-power. He would go up in brief flares of nervous excitement, and burn out as quickly, like a fire of straw. He judged that it would be fairly safe to give him his head and let him pelt away at his new scheme because the first burst would exhaust him, and the new toy would be broken and thrown aside.

He thought of Mona. He did not anticipate much danger there. Hugh Paston was probably accustomed to highly decorative females; he did not think his little brown mouse would be classed as a female at all in Paston's eyes.

His visitor suddenly broke in on his thoughts, and in the odd way he had done two or three times before, he voiced the very thing that the old bookseller had been turning over in his mind.

'Jelkes, can we run this show with men only, just you and I, or shall we want some women?'

Jelkes grunted non-committally.

'Got your eye on any women for the job?'

'I know of plenty who'd like to join the – er – witchcoven when we get it going, but I don't know of any who'd be any use as priestesses. But I know various folk connected with the stage, and I thought we'd probably be able to find a young actress of the right type, one of these classical dancers, you know, and teach her the job, and she could teach the others.'

Jelkes heaved a sigh of relief. That solved one of his problems anyway.

'If you can find the right sort of priestess, I think I can lay my hands on the right sort of artist.'

'That's fine. I really feel we're getting under way. T.J., I'll be a different man if I have something to do, and feel that I'm really getting somewhere instead of chasing my tail in circles down the arches of the years. Now then, let's get down to practical politics. What's the first move? Find a house?'

'No, not quite, the first move is to decide exactly what you want to do, and then see how we can best set about doing it.'

'We, T. Jelkes? Did I hear you say "we"? You impenitent old heathen, I believe you're getting quite keen on the scheme.'

'I'll try anything once,' said T. Jelkes grimly. 'Now tell me straight, what are you trying to get at with your invocation of Pan and all the rest of it?'

'Well, it seems to me, T.J., that if I get Pan, I'll get all the rest of it. Now don't think that I'm suffering from delusions. I know perfectly well that no cosmic billy-goat is going to materialize on your hearth-rug: but it's my belief that if I can break out of the luminous opacity of the opal, something in me is going to touch something in the spiritual world that corresponds to it. I don't want anything spiritual, it isn't my line, I had an overdose of it at Oxford. What I want is that something vital which I feel to be somewhere in the universe, which I know I need, and which I can't lay my hand on. Now I call that "something" the Great God Pan.'

Hugh Paston, chased off to bed by the sleepy bookseller, found sleep far from him. His mind was roused to alertness by the talk of the evening in a way that it had never been roused before, and images chased each other through his brain. The house he proposed to buy and equip as a marvellous temple of the Old Gods – in fact more than a temple, a monastery, for there must be others who would delight to join him on his quest – took various forms in his imagination as the dark hours went slowly past. First it was to be of classical architecture, with a front entrance resembling the Parthenon, over the door of which Jelkes' artist friend should carve the motto: 'Know thyself'. Entering, one should find oneself in a vast pillared hall to impress the imagination. Everything was to be of white marble. Then he discarded the marble as too like a bathroom, and the house took on a designedly commonplace exterior; but as soon as the front door opened, one found oneself in the mysterious gloom of an Egyptian temple, with vast shadowy images of the gods looming over one.

He lay on his back on the feather-bed and stared up at the shadowy outline of the cock-eyed canopy, dimly revealed by the faint light that always shines through a London window, and wondered where his quest would end, if there were any end to it. He had spoken with great assurance to old Jelkes concerning his quest of Pan, but did he really believe in it himself? One thing, and one thing only he knew, he had a desperate need that was eating him up and destroying him, as if something were feeding on his tissues, and that something could only be appeased by the thing he chose to call Pan, whatever that might ultimately prove to be. It was the x in his calculation. He wasn't obliged to define it at the present moment. He could erect an altar to the Unknown God if he chose.

The fancy temples passed from his thoughts and he lay along the soft hummocks of the feather-bed wondering exactly what was going to happen now that he had deliberately and with malice aforethought unleashed the Pan Within and sent it forth in search of the Cosmic Pan. He wondered what manner of thing in reality sympathetic magic might be; as described by the anthropologists it was just plain idiocy; but he had a shrewd suspicion the anthropologists never really got at the heart of anything. In sympathetic magic one imitated a thing and so got into touch with it. How superstitious, said the anthropologists. What childishness the mind of primitive man is capable of! But Ignatius Loyola said: Put yourself in the posture of prayer, and you will soon feel like praying; and the founder of the Jesuits was reckoned a very profound psychologist.

Hugh Paston had browsed to some purposed on the tangled shelves of the dusty library. All the books that Jelkes most highly esteemed, his private library, one might say, were in the inner room, safe from sacrilegious hands, and in these Hugh had dipped and skipped extensively. It was not in his nature to work systematically; studying, annotating, collating, experimenting, as the old bookseller had done; but he was an expert at picking up the drift of a book with the minimum of reading. One thing, and not much else, he had picked out from four tattered, dog-eared, paper-backed volumes on magic spelt with a K— the magician surrounds himself with the symbols of a particular potency when he performs a magical operation in order to help himself to concentrate. That was a useful practical point, thought Hugh Paston; it bore out his theory that the sympathetic magic of Loyola's 'Exercises' could be usefully reinforced by all the deckings of a temple. And if, in addition to the decked-out temple, one lived the life – one had every object within one's sight, every garment one wore, every word one spoke, or that was spoken to one, tuned to the same key over a period of time – surely the effect would be reinforced a hundredfold?

He was determined to seek Pan by the same methods that other people use to seek Christ. Was it a horrible blasphemy? That would certainly be the opinion of most people, but he didn't mind that. Was it the Black Mass? In a way he supposed it was, and yet it did not seem to him black. He certainly had no intention of desecrating anything that anybody held sacred.

He composed himself for sleep on his back, for he had always understood that this position induced dreams, and sent his mind ranging out over the vales of Arcady in search of Pan. In his imagination he performed the 'composition of place', reconstructing the scene from what he could remember of the classics, so laboriously and unprofitably rammed into his head at Harrow. The sparse woods of oak and fir; the wine-dark sea beneath; the sound of the bees in the cistuses, the basking lizards, and above all, the flocks of leaping goats springing from rock to rock. He imagined the thin fluting pipe of the goatherd that at any moment might change to the pipes of Pan; he smelt the smell of the pines in the rare dry air; he felt the sun warm upon his skin; he heard the surf of the loud-sounding sea on the rocks far beneath. He heard the crying of gulls. Were there gulls in the isles of Greece? He did not know, he only knew he heard them; they had come of their own accord.

But the act of attention and question had broken the magic, he was back in bed again, with Greece far away, as if seen through the wrong end of an opera-glass. All the same he had seen enough to satisfy him. Those gulls had been extraordinarily real, and he hadn't phantasied them as he had the goats, he had actually heard them.

He turned over and lay passively waiting for sleep, his mind drifting idly over what he had just experienced; over his talks with old Jelkes in the dusty brown bookshop; he remembered a particular race he had run in at school, when he had been in particularly good condition; the sun had been warm on his back through the thin running singlet as he had crouched waiting for the start, just like the sun in ancient Greece. His wife's face came to him, as she sat before her mirror, making-up; her frock off, her backless scanties revealing the satiny skin with its softly-moulded muscles, so different to a mans.' She turned her head to speak to him, and he suddenly realized with a start that it was not his wife, but a stranger. But in that brief glimpse he could discern no more than a flash of eyes, nose and mouth. He could not identify the face, save that it was not his wife's.

Then he found himself out on the hillside among the thin woods of oak and fir, and ahead of him moved through the light shadow the satiny back. He followed it, springing after it; it kept ahead. He quickened his pace; he was sure that when it came out into the sunshine, as come it must in those sparse woods, he would see the face; but it did not come, and he lost sight of it, and found himself in deeper woods, a dense growth, dark with laurels. And through that darkness there came a curious cold exhilarating fear, a touch of panic.

He found himself sitting up in bed, tense and startled. Something must have wakened him suddenly. What was it? He listened, eyes staring into the darkness. His ears took in nothing, but his nose did. There was a distinct smell of burning.

He leapt out of bed, flung open his door, went out on to the landing and shouted for Jelkes. The old house would burn like tinder if it once got a start. A bump upstairs told him that the old man had roused, and the light of a candle over the banisters immediately followed.

'Jelkes?' he called out. 'I woke up smelling smoke. I think we'd better have a look round.'

Jelkes joined him, and they stood on the stairs sniffing, trying to see whether the smoke came up from below. But it didn't. They went into Paston's room, and there they met it, faint blue wreaths of it, and a very distinct smell. The old man stood still and stared at those blue wreaths revealed by the candlelight, making no attempt to do anything about it. Hugh was round the room like a questing hound; head under the bed, head in the fireplace, flinging up the window to see whether the smoke had come in from outside. But he found nothing. Still old Jelkes did not move.

'There's smoke all right,' said Hugh, shutting the window. 'But I can't trace where it's coming from.'

'No,' said Jelkes, 'and you won't either, because it isn't here.'

'Where is it then? In the next house?'

The old man shook his head. 'No, it isn't on this plane at

all. Do you notice that it is the smell of smouldering cedar-wood?'

He suddenly found himself seized by the shoulders and swung around his dusty landing in a wild dance. 'T.J.,' he cried. 'Do you realize we've made a start? We've really made a start!'

'Damn!' said T. Jelkes, as the candle fell over and spilled hot wax on his thumb.

CHAPTER THREE

Upon the two men in the old bookshop the cold light of morning had its usual sobering effect. Hugh Paston wondered how much of last night's experience was pure imagination, and T. Jelkes wondered how in the world he was going to steer between the Scylla and Charybdis that confronted him. Every dictum of common sense told him to leave well alone; he would embroil himself in a pretty kettle of fish if he went any further. Occultism was all right between the covers of books, especially novels; but in real life it would probably prove to be pretty explosive. He himself was by nature the dreamer, the contemplative; the mystical philosophy appealed to him for the understanding it gave, and as a way of escape from the limitations of life as it is lived on a meagre income. But Hugh Paston was no mystic; whatever he learnt he would immediately put into practice. Old Jelkes saw himself being dragged in out of his depth when the duckling he had hatched took to the water.

He looked at his *vis-à-vis* across the breakfast table, and saw that he was staring glumly into the fire. Hugh sighed and said: 'I shall have to tackle my mother today. Can't leave things hanging about any longer.'

Jelkes nodded. 'Back to lunch?' he inquired.

'No, back to supper – if I may.'

Having seen his guest safely off the premises, Jelkes discarded his dressing-gown for an ancient Inverness cape and sallied forth. He had not far to go. A couple of turns, and he was at his destination. He pressed one of a number of bells at the side of a shabby door under a pretentious portico. A visiting-card stuck up beside it with a drawing-pin announced that Miss Mona Wilton, Designer and Craftworker, was the owner of the bell. He heard a step on the bare tiles of the hall, the door opened, and a girl in a faded blue linen smock presented herself.

He looked at her sharply, almost suspiciously, and saw what he expected to see – a pinched look about the nostrils, a hollowness about the eyes; early in the day as it was, the girl looked fine-drawn and exhausted, and there was about her a curious air of apprehension. Jelkes blamed himself bitterly that he had not been round before to see what was happening.

At the sight of the old bookseller the girl's eyes filled with tears and she was unable to speak.

'Why didn't you come round and see me?' demanded Jelkes, glaring at her.

'I'm all right,' the girl answered, ushering him into the dusty, empty hall, whose only furniture was a smelly pram.

He followed her up the wide, uncarpeted stone staircase. Up and up they went; and presently the bare stone gave place to echoing wood and the stairs grew steeper. Each landing was decorated with milk bottles, full and empty; also ash-cans – full.

Finally they came to the narrow winding stairs that led to the attics. At the top was a flimsy, glass-panelled partition. They passed through it, and the girl closed the door behind them.

'Heavens, what a climb!' said the panting bookseller. 'No wonder you keep your figure, my dear.'

'It's worth it,' said the girl. 'You see, I can shut my door behind me and have privacy up here, and no one else in the house can. Besides, there's the view and the sunsets.'

Jelkes thought to himself that the sunsets must be poor consolation for grilling under the tiles during a London summer.

The girl led him into a little sitting-room lit by small dormer windows in the sloping walls, and placed him in the one arm-chair as the guest of honour. There was no fire in the grate, but an eiderdown that had slipped to the floor behind the chair showed how she had been keeping herself warm.

Miss Wilton sat down on a small pouf, folded her arms

round her knees – to keep herself from shivering, he suspected, and smiled up at him with a gallant attempt at cheerfulness.

'What brings you here at this time of the morning?' she inquired.

'A job of work,' said Jelkes.

Her face brightened eagerly. 'For me?'

'Yes, if you'll take it on. It's a very odd job, but I think there's money in it.'

'It will have to be very odd indeed if I don't take it on. My last paper has let me down.'

'Why didn't you tell me?'

'Oh, well, one can't tell that sort of thing, can one? You haven't got much more than I have, you know.'

'I've got enough to give you a meal,' said Jelkes savagely.

'Well, as a matter of fact, I did look round last night, but you had got someone with you, so I did not come in.'

Jelkes snorted, and rose to his feet resolutely.

'You are coming round with me now to have a meal,' he said, 'and you'll get no information till you do.'

'Well, Uncle Jelkes, I won't say no. I've done about as much slimming as I care for.'

She hung the smock up on a peg behind the door, appearing in a shabby brown jumper and skirt that emphasized the sallowness of her skin and the dullness of her dark hair; put a little knitted cap on her head; pulled on a brown tweed coat with a worn coney collar, and slipped her latch-key into her pocket.

Jelkes, looking at her, felt relieved. It was improbable that Paston would get into mischief in that quarter.

They went round to the bookshop, and Jelkes warmed her by his fire, and filled her with sausages and tea, till the fine-drawn look gradually faded from her face and she settled down in the corner of the sofa that Hugh Paston had made his own, and helped herself to one of his cigarettes.

'Well now, what about this job?'

'Yes, what about it?' said Jelkes, scratching what was left of his hair. 'I hardly know where to begin. It's a fellow that wants a house furnishing.'

'You mean he wants me to design the decorations, and choose the furniture, and generally see the job through?'

'Yes, that's it,' said the bookseller hesitatingly.

'And the rest?' said Miss Wilton. 'You're looking very guilty, Uncle Jelkes. Isn't this individual respectable?'

'Yes, yes, he's all right. At least I hope so. I suppose you can take care of yourself as well as any other girl of your age.'

'If I couldn't,' said Mona, 'I'd have become extinct long ago. I'll keep my end up with this individual as long as he's solvent. But I don't want to let any firms in for bad debts, because that will queer my pitch for next time.'

'He's solvent right enough. He's the grandson of the man that founded Paston's, the big tea merchants. I suppose it practically belongs to him, and a lot more beside.'

'Is he anything to do with that man whose wife was killed in a motor smash just recently when she was eloping?'

'Yes, it's the same man. But she wasn't eloping. No such luck. She was keeping two homes going.'

'I call that a dirty trick.'

'An uncommonly dirty trick. And it's made a nasty mess of the man. I'm exceedingly sorry for him. He has now put his house and furniture in the auctioneer's hands, lock, stock, and barrel.'

'And he wants me to fit him up with a new one? That ought to be interesting.'

'Very interesting,' said Jelkes drily. 'I only hope it won't be too interesting by the time you're through with it.'

'What is all the mystery? Do come to the point, Uncle.'

'Well now, I'll tell you, Mona. He's been dipping into Huysmans' books, *A Rebours* and *Là-Bas*, and he wants to amuse himself by going and doing likewise.'

'Does he want to work the Black Mass? How entertaining!'

'Now, Mona, I won't have you talking like that, even in fun. He certainly isn't going to work the Black Mass or I wouldn't have put you on to him. What he wants to do is to furnish a house on – er – esoteric lines.'

'What exactly does he understand by that?'

'Hanged if I know. And I don't believe he does, either.'

41

'Is he handsome?'

'No. Plain as a pikestaff.'

'Are you nervous for my morals, Uncle Jelkes?'

'No more than usual, my dear. But you know what these society men are.'

'Oh, well, I'll soon disillusion him. By the way, where is his house?'

'He hasn't decided yet. I believe you will be wanted to help with the house-hunting.'

'Uncle, this is going to be fun. I've never had a chance to choose the house before. I've always had to make the best of what someone else has chosen.'

'It will be more than fun, Mona. It will be a really useful piece of work if you handle him the right way. The fellow wants taking out of himself or I really think he will go on the rocks.'

'When am I to meet the poor young man? I take it he's young, or you wouldn't be so apprehensive about my morals.'

'You come round this evening about seven and have a spot of supper with us. And put on that green frock of yours.'

Miss Wilton had hardly got out of the door when in came Hugh Paston.

'Well, T.J.,' he said, 'I've done my duty by my family. I've lunched with my mother. Poor old mater. She's terribly fed up about this business. She can't exactly blame me, and yet she's furious with me. She said I ought to have looked after Frida better.'

The old bookseller grunted his disapproval. 'I've seen that artist I told you of.' He handed Hugh Mona's professional card.

'Oh, a woman?' said Paston.

'Yes. Plain, Thirtyish. Competent. You'll find her all right. She knows her job. She's coming in this evening to supper.'

Jelkes was busy dishing up the ready-made beefsteak pudding, which was half in and half out of its basin when there

42

came a sound of knocking on the half-glass door of the shop.

'Go to the door, will you, Hugh?' he called from the kitchen. He heard footsteps crossing the oilcloth floor of the shop, the clang of the bell as the door opened, and voices – the man's pleasantly cordial, the woman's impersonal and business-like.

Mona Wilton, coming in hatless through the door of the shop, was surprised to find herself confronted by a stranger. She saw before her a loosely-built man whose well-cut suit did what it could towards disguising his stooping shoulders. His sharp-featured face looked haggard, and his black tie reminded her why. Except for his good clothes he was a nondescript individual, she thought, lacking personality. She was not surprised that this man's wife had been unfaithful to him. What was there in him to hold a woman faithful?

He, on his side, saw a youngish woman, tired-looking, with a sallow complexion and rather unkempt dark hair. She had a square face, with a strong jaw and wide mouth, innocent of lipstick. The only thing that struck him about her was the strong, muscular neck, the muscles showing moulded like a man's under the olive skin. She had hazel eyes, set wide apart under heavy black brows that almost met over the bridge of the short, straight nose. Her brows were much blacker than her hair, which was a rusty brown, like the coat of an ill-kept cat. She wore it *coupé en page*, with a straight-cut fringe in front, and a straight-cut bob behind.

She went through into the room behind the shop, and as he lingered behind to secure the door, he heard her being grunted at by the bookseller. He was not particularly struck with Jelkes's choice. In fact, to be candid, he was disappointed. He had hoped for something much more exotic than this. She looked competent, however; and there would obviously be no nonsense about her.

He joined the party in the room behind the shop. Jelkes wasted no time in introductions. He took it for granted they had become acquainted. They drew their chairs up to the table, and he ceremoniously laid before them an old willow-pattern dish, burnt almost black in the oven, instead of serving the food out of the usual frying-pan.

43

Conversation was stilted. Old Jelkes did not bother with it, but shovelled down his food in silence, as was his usual custom. Hugh Paston tried to get the girl to talk about her work, and this she did impersonally and without enthusiasm, telling him what her qualifications were, and what experience she had had. He saw that she was not prepared to make friends, but was keeping him on a purely business footing.

The meal was dispatched expeditiously under such circumstances. Jelkes moved them over to the fire to drink their tea, and with an airy wave of his hand, said: 'Now, you two, get on with your business while I clear away,' and disappeared into the kitchen and left them to it.

Hugh, taking his cue from the girl's attitude, came straight to business. 'Has Jelkes told you anything about what I want doing?' he inquired.

'A little,' said the girl. And then suddenly the wide colourless lips broadened into a smile, 'I heard you have been reading *A Rebours*.'

The sudden humanizing of the girl startled Hugh Paston, she changed so completely. But before he had time to respond, her face settled back again into its impassivity.

'I suppose Jelkes had told you I'm half mad?' he said.

The smile hovered at the corners of her mouth.

'No, he didn't exactly say that,' she said.

'Well, take it from me, I am. At any rate, I'm very eccentric.'

The smile hovered again for a moment, and then suddenly the whole face changed and softened and became almost beautiful, and Hugh Paston knew that the story of his tragedy had been told to this woman. A wave of uncontrollable emotion surged up in him; his mouth quivered and his eyes stared into space, seeing his mutilated dead. It was a moment or two before he could recover control, but when he did, and met the woman's eyes again, he knew that the barriers were down between them.

He moved uneasily in his seat, seeking desperately for some remark that would serve to break the silence and bring the atmosphere back to normal.

It was the woman, however, who picked the situation out

of the fire. 'I gather that the first thing to do is to set to work and find a house?' she said. 'What sort of a house do you want, and where?'

'Do you know, I haven't the remotest idea,' said Hugh, and the girl burst out laughing. The intolerable tension was relieved, and Hugh leant back in his corner of the sofa and laughed too.

Mona Wilton leant forward, resting her elbow on her knee and her chin on her hand, and considered him.

'It is to be a mixture of *Là-Bas* and *A Rebours*, is it?' she said.

'Yes, that's exactly it,' replied Hugh eagerly.

'Does access to town, or anything like that matter?'

'Not in the slightest.'

'Very well, then, the best thing we can do is to get out a map and pick a district that will give the right conditions. Uncle Jelkes!' she called, and the old bookseller popped his head out of the kitchen. 'Have you got a big atlas? One that has a geological map in it?' Jelkes ambled over to the far corner of the room, pushed some books aside with his foot, and extracted an enormous and very dilapidated tome. 'And I want a pencil and ruler, please,'

'Huh,' said the bookseller. 'So you're at that game, are you?'

'Now look,' said Mona, opening the atlas at the map of England. 'There are certain places that are more suitable than others for what you want to do, just as there are some places where you can grow rhododendrons, and some where you can grow roses. Now look at this map. You see Avebury?'

'Yes.'

'That was the centre of the old sun-worship. Now draw a line from Avebury to any other place where there are the remains of ancient worship, and anywhere along that line will be good for what you want. If you want to wake the Old Gods, then you have to go where the Old Gods are accustomed to be worshipped.'

'But then surely one would go to Avebury itself, or Stonehenge?'

'Too much of a tourist show. You would get no seclusion. No, the lines of force between the power centres are much better for your purpose.'

'Okay. I've got my finger on Avebury, what next?'

'Bring the ruler on to Tintagel. That's the western power-centre. Now draw a line right across the map to Avebury and project your line to St Albans. Is that straight?'

'Dead straight. It's one line.'

'St Albans is the eastern power-centre. Now take St Albans Head in Dorset, and lay your ruler from there to Lindisfarne, off the Northumberland coast. Does that pass through Avebury?'

'Yes.'

'Lindisfarne is the northern power-centre. So you see, if you take a line through Avebury from either Lindisfarne or Tintagel, you end up with a St Albans. Odd isn't it?'

'Yes, it's odd. But I don't quite see why it's odd.'

'St Alban was the first British saint.'

'Look here, we don't want any saints in this business.'

'Don't you realize that these prehistoric saints are really the Old Gods with a coat of whitewash? Do you know that somewhere in the neighbourhood – sometimes actually in the crypts of the oldest cathedrals – the ones with some Saxon work in them, you invariably find traces of the old sun-worship. The old pagan Britons were in the habit of having fairs when they assembled at their holy centres for the big sun festivals. The fairs went on just the same, whether they were pagan or Christian, and the missionary centres grew up where the crowds came together. When the king was converted, they just changed the Sun for the Son. The common people never knew the difference. They went for the fun of the fair and took part in the ceremonies to bring good luck and make the fields fertile. How were they to know the difference between Good Friday and the spring ploughing festival? There was a human sacrifice on both occasions.'

' "*Plus ça change, plus c'est la même chose*",' said Hugh.

'Precisely. You see, where people have been in the habit

46

of reaching out towards the Unseen, they wear a kind of track, and it's much easier to go out that way.'

'Are the Old Gods synonymous with the Devil?'

'Christians think they are, but I think they're the same thing as the Freudian subconscious.'

'Oh, you do, do you? Now I wonder what you mean by that?'

'Shall we get on with our house-hunting? Now the best place to get the kind of experiences you want is on the chalk. If you think of it, you know, all the earliest civilization in these islands was on the chalk. Avebury's on the chalk; and St Albans is on the chalk. Anywhere on that line, where it runs through the chalk will serve your purpose.'

'That's narrowed the field of search down very satisfactorily. Now what's the next move?'

'Get a large-scale ordnance map and look for standing-stones and hammer-pools. Standing-stones are the sighting-marks on these lines of force between the power-centres. The stones on the high places, and the hammer-pools in the bottoms. Water shows up in a valley bottom among trees, where stones wouldn't. You sight from one to another, and get a dead straight line across country. You know the Long Man, cut out of the turf on the chalk downs? You remember he has a staff in each hand? Well, those are the pair of sighting-staffs that are used for marking out these lines. These lines criss-cross all over England just like a crystalline structure. You can work them out on any large-scale ordnance map by means of the place-names and standing-stones and earthworks.'

'But look here, my idea is to do an invocation of Pan. What has all this got to do with Pan?'

'Well, what is Pan? You don't suppose he's half a goat, any more than Jehovah is an old man with a gold crown and a long white beard, who made man out of mud, do you?'

'To tell you the honest truth, I've never thought about it. The one's just as much a name to me as the other. But never mind the metaphysics. Let's get on with the house.'

'But it's applied metaphysics you're aiming at.'

'I don't know anything about that either. I'm afraid it's beyond me. Now look here, what's the next item on the programme? Go house-hunting along this line of villages on the chalk? Who's going to do it?'

'I will, if you wish.'

'How will you manage about transport? Supposing I run you round in my car, and then we can look at them together?'

'That is very kind of you.'

The following day, at ten o'clock precisely, Mona Wilton presented herself at the second-hand bookshop, clad in her brown tweed coat with the coney collar and her little knitted cap. Outside the door stood an open two-seater. It had the minutest windscreen and no hood. Mona gazed at it apprehensively; her tweed coat was of the cheapest, with little warmth in it, and the day was bleak.

She entered the shop and found Hugh and the old bookseller still at their breakfast. She was offered a cup of tea, and accepted it. Hugh rose from the table and girded himself into a heavy leather motoring coat and pulled a big pair of wool-lined gauntlets on to his hands. 'Now we're ready,' he said. 'I must apologize for the car. I had forgotten I'd only got this one when I offered you transport.'

Mona remembered what had happened to the other car, and she guessed from his face that he was thinking of the same thing.

They entered the two-seater. She had a beautiful llama-wool rug round her knees, but the cold wind cut like a knife through the upper half of her as the car whipped into the main road. To her surprise, they turned east instead of west. The car twisted through the traffic like a hound, and then came to an abrupt standstill outside the magnificent premises of a firm of motor accessory dealers. Hugh Paston got out. Mona, supposing he was going to get something for the car, stopped where she was.

'Come along,' said Hugh, opening the low door for her. She got out meekly and followed him. One does not argue with clients.

He led the way through the region of lamps and horns and came out where rows of leather coats hung on stands.

'I want a coat for this lady,' he said to the shopwalker.

Mona gasped. Opened her mouth to slay him. Shut it again in bewilderment and stared at him in speechless protest. He turned to her with a melancholy smile on his face.

'Don't worry,' he said. 'This means nothing to me. I've got a lot more than I know what to do with. You can leave the coat in the car if you don't want to take it, but I can't stand watching you shiver.'

Mona could not find a word to reply. Every instinct of the independent professional woman was against accepting the gift, and yet she was profoundly touched by the way it was done. The man's manner conveyed the impression that he had not the slightest expectation of being liked for himself; that he had not the slightest expectation of receiving any gratitude for anything he might do. Before she could find her tongue, the assistant returned.

It was a very different matter, driving in the camel-lined leather coat to what it was driving in her thin little worn-out wrap. The car, roaring in second, whipped in and out of the traffic. Mona was interested in watching how Hugh Paston handled it. One can learn a great deal about a man by watching the way he handles a car. She saw that he knew exactly what he was about with a car, what he could do with it, and what he could ask of it.

She realized very clearly that the man beside her was by no means in a normal state at the moment, and wondered what he might be like when he was himself. Between his sudden flare-ups of animation he was curiously negative. She got the impression that this negativeness was his habitual attitude; and yet it did not seem to her that it could be considered normal. He gave her the impression of a man who had given life up as a bad job; and yet in his position he had only to formulate a wish in order to gratify it. Now she had been on the point of giving life up as a bad job because the struggle to keep her head above water was too severe. If she had had this man's resources, she thought, she would have lived with a most amazing fullness of life.

With a car like Hugh Paston's, and handled in the way he handled it, they were not long before they got clear of the London streets into an arterial road. Hugh changed into top gear, the car settled down to a steady snore, and conversation became possible.

'How far out shall we run before we start house-hunting?' said the man to his companion as the scanty weekday traffic thinned out behind them.

'We must run clear of London's aura,' came the answer in an unexpectedly rich speaking-voice that rang above the rush of the wind and the roar of the car without effort. 'Look, turn down one of these lanes. We'll soon get away from it now if we leave the main road.'

Hugh swung the car into a narrow by-lane that dipped to the valley bottom where a marshy stream ran amid osiers, crossed a hump-backed bridge, and began to climb steeply up the far flank of the valley. Presently they found themselves coming out on to a wide common. Everything was brown and sear up here, though first green had been showing in the hedges of the main road. The sparse growth of Scotch firs broke the sky-line; a scanty sprinkling of birches marked the wide expanse here and there, and the blackened stems of a burnt-out patch of gorse writhed as if in perpetual agony, the tins and bottles of many picnics revealed among them. It was not a prepossessing spot.

'We are still too near the main-road,' said Mona. 'This is where London slops over on a Sunday.'

They left the common behind them and dipped into another but shallower valley, little more than a depression between two ridges, and found themselves suddenly in rural England. The average picnicking motorist had gone no further than the first bit of open ground. Here was unspoiled country. They followed a winding lane between high hedges that opened every now and then to give a glimpse of ploughland. Then the ground rose again, and plough gave place to pasture. The gradient grew steeper, and pasture gave place to open common with a few geese walking about. A hamlet strung out along one side of the common, and they drew up opposite the inevitable tiny general store. Mona marched in, and was greeted by an elderly gentleman who ledged his corporation on the counter and his backside on the shelves that held his stock. His ruddy countenance was smoothly shaven. Chilly as the day was, he wore no coat. The sleeves of a spotless pale pink shirt were carefully folded above his elbows. A grey waistcoat encircled his enormous front, and round his middle was a white fringed towel such as grocers affect. Hen-food, veterinary medicines, hardware, haberdashery, stationery, tinned goods, braces, overalls, children's pinafores, a large cheese in cut, a side of bacon ditto, a canary in a cage and a cat with family occupied the shop. He seemed pleased to see them, and a smile of immense geniality creased his vast pink countenance with its perfect schoolgirl complexion. 'And what can I do for you, sir? — madam?'

'There is not much you can do for us at the moment,' said Hugh, 'except for some milk chocolate; but we are looking for a house, and were wondering if you could put us on the track of one.'

'A 'ouse, now, a 'ouse? Now what sort of a 'ouse?'

At this very reasonable question Hugh turned and looked helplessly at Mona.

'An old house, roomy, that can be modernized and adapted.'

The old man shook his head sadly. 'We only 'ad two big 'ouses about 'ere,' he said, 'and they're both schools now. But I'll tell you where you'll find a farm that's empty. Monks Farm. It belongs to old Miss Pumfrey. That's 'er 'ouse you see through the trees. She wouldn't do no repairs to it, and I reckon she'd be glad to sell it, sir.'

'That sounds promising. We might have a look at it.'

'What about water supply?' said Mona.

'Ah,' said the old gentleman, rubbing his nose. 'You're all right for that. Them old monks, they knew what they was about. You got a fine spring just above the 'ouse, and the water comes down of it's own weight.'

They followed the road as directed, and presently, in a thick belt of firs, came to a gateless gap. They turned in, and bumped their way over a sandy surface till the firs gave place to open, moorlike pasture, dotted with clumps of gorse. It all looked pretty barren. They crossed the pasture and came to another belt of firs, and saw through them the loom of whitewashed buildings. They drove through a gap in the trees, and found themselves in the farm-yard.

Round all four sides of it, with gaps here and there for ingress, ran a low, penthouse roof; rough tarred weather-boarding rose to meet it, evidently forming a long narrow cow-house or stable. Across one end of the yard was a very large barn with a very steep roof of ancient, lichen-blotched tiles. Across the side was a long range of old stone buildings, evidently used as living-quarters, dairy, store-rooms, and anything else that the work of a farm requires. It was much too large for a dwelling house, anyway. At the other end was a smaller and more roughly-built barn, evidently of later date than the rest of the buildings. A raffle of pigsties, calf-pens and cart-shelters occupied the extensive yard round which these buildings stood; the yard itself was un-paved, and must have been a quagmire in wet weather.

Everything was boarded up and fastened with enormous padlocks. All the lower windows were shuttered, so they could not get a look-in anywhere.

'Miss Pumfrey appears to be a lady of suspicious nature,' said Hugh. He fetched a large screwdriver from the car and prised up one of the boards shoring up the penthouse. The board was rotten, and almost fell off. He put his head through the gap.

'Look at that – these stables are cloisters! They're all fan-arched.'

'No, are they really? How perfectly marvellous. Do let me look.'

Hugh drew back, and Mona popped her head through the gap. 'Do you know that behind those mangers are stone-mullioned windows?'

'Are there really? This looks absolutely ideal. Let's rush off and find Miss Pumfrey.'

'You can't live on stone mullions. Let's trace the water-supply.'

They passed through a gap in the cloisters and came out in front of the house. It was a beautifully proportioned building of two storeys, rising to a high attic gable in the middle and stretching away on either side in long wings. High up under the gable was an empty niche that had evidently once held a statue. A few gloriously golden daffodils tried to make a garden against the grey stone walls, and then unfenced, barren pasture stretched away to a far belt of trees. No other human habitation, nor any sign of the work of man, was in sight. It seemed a most unpromising spot to try and do any farming.

A heavy door, just like a church door, filled a pointed arch in the centre of the long low front. High, stone-mullioned, gothic-arched windows flanked it at regular intervals. The whole effect was very ecclesiastical.

They turned the corner and found themselves beside the bigger of the two barns. 'Obviously a chapel,' said Mona, pointing to the remains of a mouldering cross on the gable-end.

They went on in their circular tour, following a path that led through the small fir-wood at the back of the house through which they had passed on their arrival. The path ended abruptly in a miniature bog.

'Well, we've found the water-supply, anyway,' said Hugh, 'only it doesn't look very wholesome to me. I don't know what you think.'

'I expect there's a culvert somewhere that's blocked up or broken down,' said Mona. 'The water's all right, look how clear it is; and this bog hasn't been here very long; it hasn't killed the grass.'

'Well, I think we've seen as much as we can expect to see unless we commit a burglary. Shall we go back and call on Miss Pumfrey?'

As they returned down the road to the village they saw the grocer standing outside the door of his shop waving what looked in the distance like an agricultural implement, but which, as they drew nearer, proved to be a huge key.

'I've seen Miss Pumfrey,' he cried as they came within

53

hailing-distance. 'She'll sell. But don't you give 'er too much. It's all falling to bits, and as bare as the back of your 'and.'

They took the key, and returned. The great ecclesiastical door creaked open unwillingly, and they entered. The place smelt musty. Unswept stone flooring stretched away on either hand, and what had once been large barn-like rooms had been roughly partitioned with heavy boards plastered with wall-paper. A fine stone staircase wound up in a wide spiral opposite the door. They mounted it, and found themselves in a broad passage that ran the whole length of the upper storey of the building. Out of it opened a number of small low doorways.

'The monks' cells!' said Hugh.

They entered one that had evidently been used to store apples, to judge by the smell of it.

'Why, there's no window,' said Mona, 'only a little grating up near the ceiling. They must have been a very austere order indeed.'

Up again there led a small, narrow stone stair, winding in the thickness of the wall. Up this they went. At the top was a miniature church door, they pushed it open and entered, and found themselves in what had obviously been a small chapel.

'There's a queer feeling in here!' said Hugh.

'That's all right,' said Mona. 'You needn't worry about that.'

They descended to the ground-floor again, and saw cellar steps leading down into the depths.

'We'd better have a look down here,' said Mona. 'This will tell us whether the place is dry or not.'

They found themselves in a large groin-roofed cellar around three sides of which were low arched doorways, similar to the cell-doorways on the upper floor.

'Good Lord,' cried Hugh, 'those are prison cells!'

'No wonder the place has a funny feel,' said Mona. 'It must be a penal house belonging to one of the old monasteries.'

'What in the world's that?'

'Some of the monasteries were as big as small towns. Naturally not all the monks were saints. They generally used to keep one priory where they sent the monks who wouldn't behave themselves so that they shouldn't corrupt the others. Sometimes the monks were just mad and harmless. Sometimes they were – not harmless. Do you think you will be able to stand the feel of this place?'

'Why? What's wrong with it? It only feels melancholy to me.'

'It feels queer – uncommonly queer – to me, but not inimical. Let's go and see Miss Pumfrey and find out its history.'

The house whose chimneys the grocer had indicated proved to be a Georgian structure, imposing, but much in need of paint. An elderly parlour-maid opened the door. The drawing-room into which they were shown contained some very fine old furniture, but the coverings were threadbare. There was no fire, and the maid made no gesture of lighting one.

A lady entered. She wore a sagging tweed skirt; a flannel shirt-blouse; a baggy, home-knitted jersey coat, and a pair of gold pince-nez. Her greying hair was twisted into a jug-handle at the back of her head and she wore a curled fringe.

She greeted them coldly, did not ask them to sit down, and inquired their business.

'I am looking for a small property about here,' said Hugh. 'I have just seen Monks Farm, and I think it might be suitable. May I ask the price?'

'I really could not say,' said Miss Pumfrey. 'That is a matter for my solicitor.'

'Are you willing to sell?'

Miss Pumfrey hesitated. 'I should prefer to let,' she said.

'I do not wish to rent a place. I prefer to buy,' said Hugh, and he named a price that made Miss Pumfrey's eyes glisten.

They found Mr Watney the solicitor, as directed, and he proved to be a sprightly old gentleman who had a twinkle in his eye as he talked to them. He did not say very much, however, until Hugh had handed over to him a cheque for a hundred as deposit. Then he opened out.

'It is a custom with country lawyers to seal a land-deal with a glass of port. I have often wondered whether it is a relic of a Christian sacrament or a pagan libation, but I have never been able to discover. Some odd old customs linger on in the law. Did you know that when a case is settled out of court, the brief is always marked with the Sign of the Cross?'

'I know there's an odd scribble on it,' said Hugh.

'Well, that is actually the Sign of the Cross. And did you know that no priest can be a barrister? If a parson wants to change his cloth, he has to give up his orders. We got rid of the domination of the Church, but we kept the blessing on a settled case. Odd, isn't it?'

'You are interested in archaeology?'

'Yes, very. In fact I am the president of our local archaeological society. The country round about here is most fruitful ground. We have Saxon, Roman and ancient British remains in layers one below the other.'

'Can you tell me anything about Monks Farm?'

'Dear me, yes, I can tell you a lot. It is one of our most interesting relics. There are some very curious stories attached to it. Do you know we had an inquest there once, on the bones of a monk who was found walled up in the cellar? Most interesting. I was able to identify him. He was a very famous sub-prior of the parent foundation. A friend of Erasmus, at any rate he corresponded with him. He was one of the first Englishmen to study Greek?'

'What was his offence?'

'I've no idea. It must have been something pretty scandalous because there is not a word about it in the records of the monastery. Merely a remark that he was replaced in his office by someone else. No reason given. It must have been something they did not care to put on record. Monks Farm, you know, was a kind of penitentiary. Bread and water and peas in their shoes, I believe. They had a lot of trouble at that monastery. We have never been able to find out what it was all about. The records have some very odd silences. Men removed from their offices and no reason given. A new abbot appointed by the Pope instead of being elected by the monks. Then a lot of monks distributed among the other houses of the Order and all the new officials brought in from outside. A clean sweep, as it were. But there were a number of monks who weren't accounted for. They weren't sent to other houses, their names just disappeared off the rolls. We've accounted for one of them, however, at our inquest, so perhaps the others went by the same route. You may find some interesting things if you excavate.'

They drove back to town in the gathering dusk, and landed in upon Mr Jelkes just as he was getting his tea.

'Well, T.J., we've done the deed. We've bought a house.'

'You haven't been long about it,' said the old man. 'I hope you've not been rash. What have you let him in for, Mona?'

They gave him all the details, and old Jelkes nodded grimly. 'They had a lot of trouble at that particular Abbey. One of the big Catholic historians made a valiant attempt to whitewash it of recent years. You think what it must have meant to these monks, shut up in their monasteries, when they got to work on the Greek manuscripts that the Renaissance brought to Europe. Supposing they got hold of the *Bacchae*, for instance, with the invocations to Dionysus? That must have livened up the cloister a bit. This prior, Ambrosius, I believe his name was, is known to have corresponded with Erasmus. His letters are extant. There is a letter from him about the purchase of a batch of Greek manuscripts for the Abbey library. The abbot was a very old man, in his dotage, I gather, and this Ambrosius practically ran the place. A prior is the second in command, you know. Then the Pope sent a visitor to have a look at them. That made them wild, for they had a special charter that made them exempt from inspection, and they chucked the visitor out. But the next thing was that the Pope sent them a new abbot, and the civil power enforced it. The old abbot was dead and Ambrosius was expecting to get elected. But he never was. He just disappeared and they got an Italian in charge of them. Then there was that clean sweep you've been hearing about. Something pretty bad went wrong with that monastery.'

'Do you suppose that poor old Ambrosius was playing about with an invocation of Pan?'

'How do I know? All I've read is the whitewashing and the reprint of the records. In come the manuscripts, and up goes the monastery. We know what Greek literature is like, and we know what monasteries are like. Then we find the smart young prior who worked on the manuscripts bricked up in a lonely grange, and we smell sulphur.'

'Was he a young chap?'

'He was about your age, Hugh, when he disappeared off the map.'

'Poor devil, he has my sympathy. I wouldn't have fancied being bricked up with the best part of my life before me.'

Sleepy from the fresh air, Hugh got off to bed early. But sleepy as he was, he determined to try and recapture the trail of the previous experience. He felt somehow that he must do this thing regularly if he were to succeed with it. He turned on to his back, crossed his arms on his chest, and called up before his mind's eye the picture of a sunny hillside above the sea in ancient Greece. But before he knew where he was, he was sliding off into dreamland.

It seemed to him that he was lying on his back on a narrow plank bed. It was pitch dark, and the roof seemed to be pressing down on him and the walls closing in on him. And all the time he could hear the tolling of a bell. He felt a hood of some coarse woollen material like serge around his head, and folds of coarse serge material under his hands that were folded on his breast. In his dream he sat up on the narrow plank bed and pushed the hood off his head to wipe the sweat from his face. He passed his hand over his sweat-soaked hair, and found a round bald patch on the top of his head, as if the thick hair had been shaved away. Then in his dream he lay down again and drew the hood over his face, and concentrated his mind on one idea – to die with dignity and without struggling. Then it seemed to him that the sound of the tolling bell became merged in the beating of his own heart. The heavy beats grew louder and louder, and slower and slower, and then, all of a sudden, he found himself in the fresh air and full sunlight on the Grecian hillside, and ahead of him was the figure of the woman with the satiny back and softly moulded muscles.

He leapt after her. Round his loins was a goatskin, he could feel the rough hariness of it, but the upper part of his body was bare. The woman ahead had a fawnskin slung over her shoulder. She had an olive skin and her body was strong and muscular. In particular was he struck by the strong firm column of the neck. He pursued, but she did not so much flee as go on ahead of him.

Suddenly sleep left him, and he woke up to find himself in a bath of sweat.

CHAPTER FOUR

Real estate is not a thing that ever gets itself transferred from one owner to another expeditiously. Miss Pumfrey was not a person of whom one could ask favours in the way of obtaining possession, and Hugh reckoned he would find himself at a loose end for at least a fortnight.

At breakfast next morning he said to old Jelkes: 'What do I do about paying Miss Wilton? I'm taking up a devil of a lot of her time, and I suppose time is money with her.'

'Does she suit you?'

'Yes, first-rate. I like her.'

'Then I should put her on the pay-roll, if I were you. What are the jobs you want her for at the moment? It's too soon to start furnishing isn't it?'

Hugh was nonplussed. He hadn't thought of any particular jobs for Mona to do. What he really wanted was to get some money into her hand without hurting her pride. 'I had an idea that she might do a bit of research for me,' he said, improvising hastily. 'I'd like to trace out the history of Monks Farm.'

Jelkes nodded. 'There is sure to be a good collection of stuff in the library of the local museum. I bet there's plenty of material available for piecing together by anyone who knows as much as we do of the queer side of things.'

'Yes you're right. I'll run her down to see old Watney and we'll have a rummage round.'

Once again the racing-car took the road north with Mona Wilton, hooded and clad in green, seated beside its driver.

Mr Watney gave them a list of books to refer to, and a note of introduction to the curator at the museum, and off they went. The curator, a Mr Diss, proved to be just such another as Mr Watney, and the two were apparently cronies, being respectively president and secretary of the local archaeological society. The museum was the proud possessor of the Abbey rolls, and they had the interesting experience of looking at the actual entry of the purchase of the Greek manuscripts from Erasmus' agent. The monks had paid thirty pounds for them – a substantial sum in modern money.

The curator was called away, and left them in the hands of a youth with instructions to get them whatever they wanted. Hugh gave him the list Mr Watney had furnished, and the youth deposited a pile of books before them and disappeared.

'Now then, we'll share these out,' said Hugh. 'I'm an adept at skipping.'

They got to work, and silence fell between them, which Mona was the first to break. 'This is interesting,' she said. 'It's the ghost at the farm.'

Hugh left his chair and came round to her side of the table and sat down beside her, reading over her shoulder.

The book that was open before them concerned local superstitions. Monks Farm bore a sinister reputation. It appears that it was not originally a penal house. It had been built by the infamous prior, Ambrosius, as a special place of retreat and meditation to which certain picked monks retired at certain seasons. It was not until the trouble broke out that it was turned into a penal house by the simple expedient of blocking up the cell windows and making the monks who were there, stop there, whether they liked it or not. Ambrosius was taken to his own special priory and bricked-up below-stairs as a warning and an example. The other monks were kept in their cells on a low diet till they died more or less naturally. They never saw the light of day again. In darkness and solitary confinement they waited their end. One man lived to be over eighty – fifty-five years' imprisonment. Their jailers never spoke to them, and jailer replaced jailer till the last monk died, and then the place was abandoned. The ghost of the prior was supposed to walk round the cells, talking to his monks and consoling them.

'What do you suppose they were up to at that priory?' said Hugh. 'Raising the Devil?'

'I shouldn't be a bit surprised if they were trying to do exactly the same thing that you are trying to do— break away from their limitations and find fullness of life.'

'I don't think it would suit my style. I am out after Pan.'

'Well, aren't you approaching Pan through prayer and meditation?'

'Now you mention it, I believe I am. In fact, I tried to apply to him the Method of St Ignatius. I made a mental picture of ancient Greece, and it came alive, and for a moment I found myself there. And then, last night, when I tried to do it again, I was too sleepy to keep control, and I dreamt of poor old Ambrosius. Or rather, I dreamt I was walled-up, like him, and very unpleasant it was, too. Then I bust out of that dream on to the Greek hillside in the sunshine, and someone was going up the hill ahead of me, and I believe it was you. At any rate, it was someone with your build and walk.'

'That's interesting,' said Mona noncommittally.

At that moment the curator returned. 'I am sorry to have had to leave you,' he said. 'Would you care to see the illuminated manuscripts?'

They acquiesced, and he led them to a glass case, unlocked it, raised the lid, and began tenderly to turn over the heavy vellum pages of an exceedingly fine psalter.

'This is particularly interesting,' he said, 'because all the initial letters are set in little scenes of the Abbey.'

He pointed out to them the high altar, the cloisters, the bell-tower, the great gate, the monks at work in the scriptorium. Then he turned another page, and pointed to a little picture of a black-robed monk sitting at his desk writing.

'This is the man,' he said, 'who laid the foundations of the famous library. A great scholar in his day, but died young. Life was short in those days.'

They saw a minute but diamond-clear portrait of a youngish man, round-shouldered at his desk. Sharp-featured, clean-shaven, tonsured. Mona glanced up involuntarily at the face of the man beside her, bending over her shoulder. Feature for feature, the faces were identical; even the scholarly stoop of the shoulder was reproduced.

'That was one of the priors, Ambrosius,' said the curator.

There was dead silence for a moment, Mona holding her breath and wondering what was going to come next.

Hugh broke it, and Mona thought his voice sounded rather odd.

'That's interesting,' he said. 'Can you tell me where they buried Ambrosius after they held the inquest on him?'

'Ah, now, that's a curious story. There is a small monastery in the town of the same Order as once owned the Abbey. The coroner offered the bones to them to inter in their graveyard, but they declined them, so they were buried in the churchyard in the village. Evidently Ambrosius died in bad odour. Now, if you will excuse me, I must get back to my work. Perhaps you will return these books to the desk when you have finished with them.'

Hugh took the chair Mr Diss had vacated and sat staring into space, making no attempt to start on the volume lying open in front of him. Mona, watching him, saw that he had gone very white and his eyes had a startled look in them. 'Do you know, it gave me quite a turn seeing that picture of Ambrosius. It made me realize what that bricking-up meant. Now let's have a look at this paper and see what else there is to be seen.'

' "Born in 1477",' read Hugh. ' "The illegitimate son of a huckster's daughter. Showed such marked promise in scholarship that he was admitted to the Abbey school without fee. Received the tonsure while still a youth. Was in great favour with the abbot. His rapid promotion caused much jealousy. A special mission was sent to Rome to protest against the appointment of so young a man as prior. The old abbot lived to be eighty-six, and for the last few years of his life was bedridden. Ambrosius as prior had complete control. Much jealousy ănd opposition. Ambrosius, a man of strong character, overbore the opposition and carried out his own policy. He was not a great building ecclesiastic, but he was a great scholar and collector. Much criticized for using funds to buy Greek manuscripts instead of a piece of the True Cross that was on offer to the monastery. Influence of his enemies finally prevailed with Rome after the death of the old abbot, a mission of inquiry was sent to the Abbey, and he was removed from his place as abbot-elect. Nothing further is heard of him. There is no record of his fate, death, or place of burial.

' "Although he added nothing to the structure of the Abbey, he built a daughter-house three miles away at Thorley, and there he appeared to have founded a subsidiary community of his own. Nothing is known of its nature, however, the records of this period of the Abbey's history having been destroyed in a fire which burnt out a part of the famous library, and in which perished all the Greek manuscripts purchased from Erasmus." '

'Well, that doesn't say much. I wonder who lit that fire? Their new Italian abbot, probably. I should say there is not much doubt about it that Ambrosius was up to some queer games, and the Greek manuscripts were at the bottom of the trouble. Come on, let's go home and ask Jelkes what he makes of it.'

Hugh deposited Mona at the bookshop and went to put the car away.

'Uncle Jelkes,' said Mona, as soon as he had disappeared. 'We've traced out the story of Ambrosius pretty completely, and Ambrosius was also after Pan, or something uncommonly like it. And I'll tell you another thing, we saw a little picture of Ambrosius at the museum, and it might have been a portrait of Mr Paston.'

'Damn!' said the old bookseller, and sat down in his chair with a flop. 'I knew it was going to be bad, but I never dreamt it was going to be as bad as all this!'

'Uncle Jelkes, I don't think it would take much to send Mr Paston off his head.'

'Well, my dear, we can't stop now we've started. That would make the devil of a mess. But where is the thing going to end? I've known things like this happen before. When a man who has been on the Path comes back to it again, circumstances often take him to the place of his last death.

Now we will watch and see what happens. Hugh may start recovering the memories of his last life.'

One subject, and one subject only, interested Hugh at that moment, but he found that neither Mona nor the old man were willing to talk about it. Whenever he introduced the name of Ambrosius they simultaneously and with one accord talked of something else. Hugh, who was an unsuspicious person, found this irritating. He was not sorry, therefore, to get off to bed early.

It was extraordinary the way that the recreant prior haunted his imagination; he could not get rid of him. Again and again the memory of his terrible death came back, and of the circumstances that led up to his death. From the scanty materials they had obtained, and his still more scanty appreciation of their significance, he tried to form a picture of the man's personality and of the true inwardness of his history.

He could imagine the brilliant son of the huckster's pretty but none too virtuous daughter, and wondered whether the abbot's interest in him had been genuinely paternal. It was quite likely. Rome has always taken a humane view of human nature. He could see the lad accepting the monastic life with its intellectual opportunities readily enough; throwing himself heart and soul into it in fact, and winning rapid advancement at the hands of the all-too-complacent abbot. Then he could see the sudden wakening of another side of the man's nature at the touch of Greek thought. God only knew what vivid play or daring poem had been among that job lot of Greek manuscripts purchased untranslated from Erasmus. He could imagine the tentative experimenting with some chant of invocation, and the sudden and unexpected obtaining of results, just as he himself had obtained them that night when he applied the Method of St Ignatius to the invocation of Pan. A man trained in the cloister would get results quickly and very definitely.

He could imagine the fascination of the pursuit growing on Ambrosius; the guarded sounding of others as to their fittedness for the enterprise; and then the cautious organization of the special daughter-house where the new and absorbing interest could be pursued, safe from prying eyes.

Then he could imagine suspicion gradually being aroused; the spying and watching; the gradual piecing together of the damning evidence; finally, when the death of the old abbot removed his influential protector, the sudden swoop of Rome; the clean sweep of all sympathizers; the quarantining in their own priory of those who had actually participated in the pagan rites; and the walling-up of their leader in the cellars under their feet as a terrible warning, the slow tolling of the bell informing them of the slow approach of his death. Then the long dragging years of silence and solitude and darkness till to one by one came the still slower but inevitable end. And finally the old, old man of over eighty, on whom the cell-door had shut as a lad in his twenties, found at last his release, and the priory was abandoned to the wind and the rain.

There was one gleam of light that comforted Hugh in the utter gloom of the tragedy – the return of the prior's spirit to stand by the men who had trusted him. He could imagine the shadowy figure, tall and gaunt in its heavy black habit, moving on sandalled feet along that upper corridor and pausing to talk to each monk in turn through the small barred wicket that alone remained open in the nailed-up doors of the cells. It never occurred to Hugh to ask himself how he knew that the cell-doors were nailed up.

He could imagine the amazement of the monks when first this spectral visitant greeted them through the narrow aperture; then their terror when they realized that their prior was indeed dead and that this was his ghost that had come to them. Then their gradual reassurement as they realized that the spirit was kindly – that death had in no way changed the man they had trusted. And finally, the establishment of regular communications between death-in-life and life-in-death so that the spirits of the imprisoned men rose out of the narrow confines of their cells and breathed a wider air.

Suddenly Hugh roused from his reveries to find the old bookseller standing over him, looking at him reproachfully and saying: 'Laddie, you'll set the house on fire if you go on like this.'

Hugh Paston smiled apologetically. 'Do you know, I was actually at that priory, walking up and down the passage with Ambrosius and talking to the monks? Do you realize that the fellow came back from the dead every night and talked to them? And do you know what has just occurred to me? That if he could come back to them, would it be possible to persuade him to come back for me? Now if I got hold of a good medium, do you think I could get in touch with Ambrosius?'

The old man stood looking down at him with a very queer expression on his face. 'I should leave mediums alone, if I were you, Hugh. You'll get no good from them.'

'Do you know, I believe Ambrosius would come back to me, I feel so much in sympathy with him. His history is so much like mine. I could do what he failed to do—'

A curious change came over the figure lying propped on its elbow in the bed. The rather boyish, eager, hesitating manner of a man uncertain of himself, who had never found himself, gave place to something entirely different. The air was that of a man accustomed to be obeyed. A man aloof, purposeful, resolute. The keen eyes gazed at Jelkes, but without any look of recognition in them.

'*Pax vobiscum*,' said Jelkes.

'*Et tibi, pax*,' said the man on the bed.

He looked into Jelkes' eyes for a minute, then a shudder passed through him.

Jelkes wondered how much Hugh remembered of what had happened; how far the two modes of consciousness had made any sort of contact with each other. But there was no glimmering of awareness in Hugh's rather nondescript grey-green eyes, so he bid his guest goodnight.

The next morning found Hugh perfectly normal, with no recollection whatever of the incidents of the previous night. He was all agog, however, to go down to the museum again and arrange to have the picture of Ambrosius in the illuminated psalter photographed.

Jelkes went round to fetch Mona while Hugh went to

fetch the car. 'My dear,' he said, 'we're in for the devil of a time. Ambrosius turned up last night in person.'

'What do you mean?' said Mona, startled, as much by his manner as his words.

'I went into his room last night quite by chance and found him half asleep with a lighted cigarette in his hand. He woke up and began talking about Ambrosius – I think he had been dreaming of him – and for about five seconds Hugh *became* Ambrosius, and, my God, he startled me! He didn't know me from Adam, and he looked as fierce as a hawk. I addressed him in clerical Latin, and he answered me. And then he swung back to Hugh again, and, thank God, he doesn't remember a thing about it this morning.'

'If he has done it once, he will do it again, Uncle Jelkes, especially when he gets to the farm, and what will happen then?'

'The Lord only knows. If he looks at you like he looked at me, you'll run a mile. He must have been a terror of a prior.'

Mona went up and got her leather coat and hood, and they walked round to the shop together, where they found Hugh outside on the pavement, tinkering at the car. He straightened up at their approach, and greeted them with his usual diffident air, like a schoolboy greeting his family in public – much more pleased to see them than he dared to admit.

Hugh and Mona drove off in the car and Jelkes watched them go. What was going to be the end of that also? Hugh Paston was a wealthy and well-connected man, still young, and, at the moment, very unbalanced. Mona, the daughter of a Nonconformist minister in a small manufacturing town in the Midlands, was a young woman with a stormy emotional past behind her. She had lived as girl artists breaking out from such homes are apt to live – going from one extreme to the other. Hugh had been educated at Harrow and Balliol, Mona at the local high-school. Hugh was accustomed to a very sophisticated type of femininity. If Mona managed to be clean and tidy, that was about as high as she aspired. Jelkes judged that Hugh's present mood was a reaction to the shock and disillusionment he had been through, and that when it wore off he would revert to normal and return to his own kind. He would no longer be willing to put up with the discomforts of the bookshop or the limitations of Mona's society.

At the moment Mona appeared to be taking things impassively and impersonally. Her attitude was that of a woman humouring her employer, falling in with his mood, and at the same time keeping him at arm's length. But he knew from experience that underneath her impassive exterior, Mona Wilton was a young woman of stormy emotions, and apt to get the bit between her teeth in pursuit of them. Jelkes could not quite see how romance was going to come into it, in view of all the circumstances, but all the same, he wished Hugh would give Mona a list of what he wanted and send her out to attend to it, instead of running round with her like this.

In the meantime Hugh was putting the car along in the way to which it was accustomed, and they were not long before they arrived in the little town and had sought out the photographer. They took the scrubby little man and his gear to the museum, where he did his job and departed; but Hugh, as Mona expected, remained bent over the illuminated pages of the ancient book. She watched his face as he studied them, and it seemed to her that his features changed as she watched him, taking on the same air of a watching hawk that was worn by the sharp features of the tonsured head rising from the black folds of its thrown-back cowl in the four-hundred-year-old picture. The two men were certainly extraordinarily alike, and as the living man stared at the dead one, he grew more and more like him.

It seemed to Mona as if her employer were hypnotizing himself with the picture of the dead monk, and she felt that she had better break the spell before it took altogether too much hold on him.

She leant forward, intending to touch him on the sleeve, but the leg of her chair slipped on the uneven floor, and instead she touched him on the bare skin of his wrist. He looked up suddenly, and met her eyes, and the man who looked up was not Hugh, but Ambrosius, and he had reacted

69

to her touch as a cloistered monk might be expected to react. Mona found herself looking into the eyes of a bird of prey.

She knew well enough that she had Ambrosius and not Hugh Paston to deal with, but she had no means of knowing whether the monkish celibate was infuriated by her touch, or stirred out of all reason by it. She was alone with him in a large empty upper room of the medieval house that served the town as a museum. From the ordinary point of view she was dealing with a madman – a man who imagined himself to be a dead and gone monk of sinister history. She was not even sure if a man of his epoch would understand modern English if she spoke to him – he must be a coeval of Chaucer. Not knowing what to do, she very wisely did nothing. The eminent churchman, whether real or imaginary, was unlikely to resort to any sudden violence or unseemliness.

Fra Ambrosius – it was impossible to think of him as Mr Paston – stared at her with the fixity of a snake at a bird. It was probable that he was just as much surprised as she was by the encounter. The room would appear familiar enough to him – it was a room of his own period, carefully preserved and restored; the book under his hand was one of his own books. The table on which it rested was a refectory table out of the monastery itself. The only thing, beside Mona herself, that was out of the picture was a notice on the wall requesting people not to smoke – a request which could have conveyed nothing to him even if he were able to decipher the modern script.

But he was not paying any attention to notices. He was entirely occupied in attending to what was before him. Mona in the vivid green of the dyed leather was sufficiently incongruous to eyes accustomed to the crude dyes of the Middle Ages. She had an elfin face at the best of times, and in her quaint green hood she looked even to modern eyes, accustomed to freakish fashions, like something strayed from the greenwood – how must she have appeared to the cloistered eyes of the ecclesiastic, accustomed to the soberly coifed heads of the medieval women, and only to those at a distance?

As she watched him, Mona saw the expression of stupefaction with which he had first greeted her gradually give place to a look of exaltation, as if he had been vouchsafed some miraculous, other-world vision. Mona wondered whether he was under the impression that he was having a vision of a saint. But the expression in his eyes disillusioned her. She thought of the Temptation of St Anthony, and wondered how Ambrosius was in the habit of dealing with devils. Was she going to be exorcised or strangled? Was Ambrosius going to do his duty as a monk and say: 'Get thee behind me, Satan?' or was he not?

She felt, from the amazed, exalted expression with which he was regarding her, that he did not believe her to be of any earthly nature, and had jumped to the conclusion that she was something come to him from another world in answer to his ungodly experiments with the Greek manuscripts. To say that Ambrosius was agitated would have been but half the truth. The medieval mind of the man returned from the dead knew no half-lights or compromise in the doctrines of sin and hell. According to all the standards of his world, he had sold his soul to the Devil and an eternity of hell-fire awaited him.

The minutes went by, and neither of them moved. Mona, watching the expressions following each other on the face of the man bending towards her – the face of a stranger though the features were familiar – had a profound realization of the tragedy of the cloister for those who have no vocation for it. The tragedy of Abélard and Héloïse. Was this an English Abélard who was bending down to look into her face across the narrow table?

She gazed back at him. The minutes were slipping away one after the other. A town clock chimed the hour. How much longer were they going to stay like this? She dared not move lest God knew what should be let loose upon her. She could conceive of Hugh Paston falling dead if the occupant of his body withdrew suddenly. Come what might, the first move must not come from her.

Then the man, without taking his eyes off hers, slowly stretched his hand and touched the back of hers with the tips of his fingers, as if feeling her pulse. The finger-tips were icy cold. It was indeed like the touch of the hand of the dead. Mona did not stir, but continued to hold his eyes with hers. He was evidently trying to ascertain whether she was flesh and blood or phantasy. He had probably known many such phantasies.

Then the other hand began to move and came towards her. Mona could see it coming, though she never took her eyes from those that gazed into hers unwavering with their bird of prey regard. What was that hand going to do? Was it coming for her throat? But no, it came to rest on her shoulder. Then the figer-tips that had rested so lightly on the back of her hand closed round her wrist. Mona could not move now if she wanted to.

So firmly had the phantasy of Ambrosius taken hold on her imagination that the modern dress disappeared from her view, and this man bending over her actually was to her the renegade Churchman, desperately risking hell-fire. Instinctively, unthinkingly, her free hand went out and rested on his arm in a touch of sympathy. She watched the eyes of the renegade, imaginary monk slowly fill with tears. It made no difference whether the man before her were a dead man come back from the past, or whether it was a madman phantasying the tragic history, the results were the same, and sprang from the same roots in frustrated human needs. Whether it were Ambrosius vowed to the celibacy of the cloister, or Hugh Paston wasting his manhood in a loveless marriage – the same causes were producing the same effects.

What would have been the end of the encounter, heaven only knew, but a step was heard on the stairs and the man hastily let go of Mona and rose upright, the keen, commanding air telling Mona that it was still Ambrosius who was present. The footsteps crossed the bare boards of the landing and came in at the doorless arch, and Mona turned to greet the curator, wondering how in the world the situation was to be carried off.

But as she turned, the spell broke, and a startled exclamation from Mr Diss caused her to turn again, to see Hugh Paston swaying with closed eyes, and then go over backwards with a crash.

They rushed round the table, but before they could get to him, Hugh was sitting up, rubbing the back of his head where it had made contact with the floor-boards.

'Good Lord, what's the matter?' he demanded, looking at them dazedly.

Mr Diss was thoroughly alarmed. 'My dear sir, allow me to assist you. Sit down a moment, and I will get you some brandy from across the way.'

Hugh, nothing loath, sat down and blinked at Mona.

'What happened?' he asked, as soon as Mr Diss's back was turned. 'Did I faint?'

'I think you must have done,' said Mona.

'That's odd. What did I faint for? I was feeling perfectly all right.'

'How are you feeling now?'

'A bit swimmy. As if nothing were real and I didn't know quite where I was. I shan't be sorry for the old boy's brandy.'

But Hugh did not get his brandy as quickly as he might have done, for Mr Diss dispatched the youth for it, and then got busy on the phone to Mr Watney.

'I wish you would come round,' he said. 'Your new client has just gone off in a dead faint, and I think the young lady is badly frightened.'

Consequently when the brandy arrived, it was brought upstairs by the pair of them, and they jointly stood over Hugh, now thoroughly ashamed of himself, while he drank it. They likewise gave a dram to Mona, for which she was truly thankful. Every time she looked at Hugh's shy, non-descript face, she felt that at any moment the burning eyes of Ambrosius might stare out at her from it.

It was immediately decided that all four of them should go round to Mr Watney's house and have some lunch before Hugh undertook the drive back to town.

During the short walk Mr Watney contrived that Mr Diss should walk with Hugh while he himself companioned Mona. 'Does Mr Paston suffer with his heart?' he asked.

'I have no idea,' said Mona. 'I only know him very slightly.'

'You are not a relation, then?'

'Oh dear no, I am a professional designer. It is my job to design all the decorations for the house and see the contracts through. I know nothing whatever of Mr Paston personally. I only met him a couple of days ago.'

'Dear, dear. Rather a trying experience for you, my dear young lady.'

'It was, very,' said Mona. 'However, he does not seem much the worse for it.'

'It is very dangerous for him to drive a car if he is subject to these attacks.'

'Yes, it certainly is,' said Mona, wondering what Ambrosius would make of modern traffic if he suddenly appeared when Hugh was at the wheel.

'Can you not persuade him to employ a chauffeur?'

'It is none of my business, Mr Watney. I can't interfere in a thing like that. I only know Mr Paston very slightly. If he chooses to take risks, that is his look-out.'

She felt that Mr Watney was probing to discover the nature of the relationship between them, and so she diligently emphasized its casualness and her total indifference to Hugh's fate.

'It may be a very unpleasant matter for you, not to say a dangerous one, my dear young lady, if you go driving about in that car of his with him.'

'Business is business, Mr Watney. I cannot dictate to my clients.'

He appeared satisfied as to Mona's entirely utilitarian interest in Hugh Paston. They came out of a narrow passage and found themselves in the Abbey close. Mona's heart was in her mouth as they crossed it lest Ambrosius should put in another appearance, but though he stared up hard at the ancient towers, nothing happened, and they reached the low ivy-covered house looking on to the monks' graveyard in safety.

It was a house of great interest and charm and contained a wonderful collection of antique furniture; but although Mona was a connoisseur of fine furniture, she had no eyes for it, for she was all the time obsessed by the idea that Hugh Paston was Ambrosius, and she could not get out of her mind the way that Ambrosius had looked at her. She could see those burning eyes still, whenever she looked at Hugh. She also saw that he had noticed that she was upset and nervous with him, and that in its turn made him nervous with her.

It was obvious that Hugh was still dazed and hardly knew what he was doing. Not only had he been through a startling psychic experience, but he had also had a good hard crack on the head. Mona felt that if Ambrosius looked at her out of Hugh's eyes again, she would rush from the room, so terrific an impression had the renegade prior made upon her. She could not keep herself from watching Hugh all the time in case he should suddenly turn into Ambrosius again. Mr Diss and Mr Watney did not increase Mona's peace of mind by endeavouring to entertain them with tales of the Abbey. They never got actually on to the subject of Ambrosius, however, for which she thanked heaven, but as every time they came anywhere near it she held her breath.

Finally the meal came to an end, and Mona took her place beside Hugh in the car, and they turned homeward.

He took the car out of the difficult streets of the town without speaking. Then he pulled in to the roadside and stopped the engine.

'I'm sorry,' he said. 'I am afraid I gave you a scare. I've never behaved like that in my life before. I suppose I must be run down after all I've been through.'

Mona had all she could do to refrain from bursting into tears. The one thing of all others she desired to avoid was being alone with Hugh in a lonely place where he might suddenly turn into Ambrosius.

'It is quite all right,' she managed to say at length, 'as long as you are not hurt.'

'I'm all right,' said Hugh, 'except for a bump on the back of my head. It is you I am worried about. I am afraid I have upset you.'

'It isn't that. I – I think I have got one of my headaches coming on.'

He started up the engine and they travelled home in silence, the headache gradually taking hold on Mona till she

75

felt as if her skull were held in a vice while knives went through her brain. By the time they arrived back at the bookshop she looked ghastly. Hugh looked at her as he helped her out of the car, and was horrified at her appearance.

'I wonder what in the world Jelkes will say to me for bringing you home like this,' he said, 'I can only say how sorry I am, Mona.'

Mona was too far gone to notice that he put his arm round her as she walked unsteadily into the shop.

Old Jelkes, wrapping up books, raised his eyebrows at the sight of the pair of them.

'I am afraid I've brought you back a wreck,' said Hugh to him.

'Got one of her headaches? Well, that's no fault of yours,' said the old man.

'I am afraid it is my fault,' said Hugh. 'I distinguished myself by fainting, and scared her to death.'

'Good Lord, are you given to that sort of thing?'

'Never done it in my life before, and don't know why I did it now.'

'Well,' said the bookseller, looking at Mona, 'I suppose it's tea and aspirin, and so to bed?'

She walked into the room behind the shop without answering, and dropping down into his own arm-chair, huddled herself over the fire.

'Let me take your coat off, my dear,' said the old man.

'No, I don't want to take it off just yet, I'm cold.'

Jelkes went off to put the kettle on for the inevitable tea and Hugh stood staring miserably at Mona, feeling himself to be responsible for her state.

Mona had not been huddled over the fire many minutes before she suddenly flung off the heavy leather coat that she had been hugging around her. 'I'm boiling hot,' she said peevishly. But in a few moments she wanted it on again. Hugh put it over her shoulders as she groped for it, and as he did so, discovered that she was shaking in a violent fit of the shivers.

He went quietly into the kitchen to Jelkes. 'This is something more than a headache. It looks unpleasantly like pneumonia to me.'

Jelkes whistled. 'That's a nasty job if it is,' he said. 'But it may only be one of her headaches. She has uncommon bad ones. I'll have a look at her. I'll soon know. I've seen plenty of her headaches.'

He returned with the tea. 'Well, lassie?' he said. 'How are you feeling?'

'Rotten,' said Mona. 'I think I've got a chill as well as a headache.'

'I think we had better put you to bed and get your doctor to you,' said Jelkes.

'Look here,' said Hugh, 'what about a nursing-home?'

'No!' said Mona, suddenly waking up. 'I'm not really bad. I'm just chilled on top of my headache, I shall be all right in the morning. I'll go home as soon as I've drunk my tea.'

'Oh no, you won't,' said the old bookseller. 'You'll stop here.'

'Quite right,' said Hugh, 'and I have a suggestion. Let me ring up my housekeeper, Mrs Macintosh, she's a good sort, and let's get a bed and whatever's needful, and shove them in your front room, and keep Mona here till we know what's wrong with her, and let Mrs Macintosh tackle the situation.'

'You won't, you won't!' cried Mona hysterically. 'I am going round to my own place. I don't want to stop here.'

'She's always like this when she has a headache,' said Jelkes aside to the agitated Hugh. 'Go on and phone your housekeeper while I keep her quiet.'

Mona rose to her feet unsteadily. 'I'm going home,' she said. How could she explain to these two men that she would not dare to close her eyes in the same house with Hugh Paston lest suddenly she should find herself in the presence of Ambrosius? Involuntarily she raised her eyes to Hugh's, and he saw the fear in them.

'Look here,' he said quietly. 'I believe she is scared that I'll treat her to another faint if she stops here. If I clear out, will you stop? I can easily go to a hotel.'

'Oh no, it's not that. It's too ridiculous.'

'Well then, what is it, Mona?' said Jelkes.

'It's nothing. I'm just being silly. I wish you'd let me go home quietly. I shall be quite all right.'

'We're not going to let you go home in the state you're in. Will you stop if Hugh clears out?'

'Yes, yes, I'll stop. There's no need for him to clear out. I'm just being silly. Don't take any notice of me. I get like this when I have a headache. I'll be all right presently.' She huddled up into a heap in the big chair and hid her face miserably in the dirty cushion.

'Go on and get your phoning done,' said Jelkes to Hugh, and Hugh vanished.

'Well, lassie, what really is the matter?' said Jelkes to Mona as soon as Hugh had departed.

'He turned into Ambrosius,' said Mona huskily.

'I thought as much,' said Jelkes.

'He – he just looked at me for ever such a long time without moving, and then someone came into the room, and he fell over backwards in a faint and woke up normal.'

'That wasn't a faint, it was the change-over from Ambrosius back to Hugh. What are you scared of, lassie? Did you find Ambrosius alarming?'

'Yes, terrifying.'

'Well, well, I don't suppose he'll do it here. Anyway, you'll have that Scottish housekeeper of his with you, and I'll keep an eye on Hugh. You ought to know enough not to be scared of the dead, Mona. A dead man's no different to a living one, except that he hasn't got a body.'

'It's not that, I'm not scared of the dead, any more than you are. It's – it's Ambrosius I'm scared of.'

Hugh Paston returned. 'O.K. She's coming round forthwith.'

'I'll get a fire going upstairs,' said Jelkes, and signalling to Hugh to follow him, he led the way out of the room. He knew Mona would not want to be alone with him.

'Look here,' he said, as soon as the fire was under way, 'don't talk to her about Ambrosius, he's got on her nerves.'

'Does she think he'll come back from the dead and chase her?'

78

'Yes, that's it.'

'Do you know, T.J., I've had an awfully strong feeling myself that he's about somewhere, but I don't think he's inimical. I think the poor devil had a rotten time and would be glad of a kind word from anybody.'

'That's all right,' said the old bookseller, 'but don't do it while Mona's seedy, or she'll go all to pieces. You keep your mind off Ambrosius while you're in this house. We don't want him manifesting here.'

CHAPTER FIVE

Mrs Macintosh arrived, and without fuss or comment, took charge of the whole situation.

'What about getting Dr Johnson?' said Hugh.

'Certainly not,' was the reply. 'If that man comes into the house, I go out of it.'

'Good Lord, what's the matter with him? Mrs Paston always thought no end of him.'

'I know she did. But he's not coming near Miss Wilton, all the same. What we want is a good, sensible, reliable general practitioner. I know exactly the man.'

When he arrived he looked like a pocket edition of old Jelkes. While he was examining the patient, Mrs Macintosh joined Hugh downstairs.

'Mr Paston,' she said quietly. 'It would be much easier for me to deal with things if you would tell me frankly what the position is.'

'There's not much to tell, Mrs Macintosh. I came across Mr Jelkes quite by chance when I was feeling rotten after the funeral, and I've been stopping with him ever since. He pulled me round a pretty nasty corner. I think I'd have gone smash if it hadn't been for him. Miss Wilton is a protégée of his. She's an artist. I have been setting to work to get another house, and I wanted the furnishing and decorating done, and Jelkes put me on to her for the job. It's her line of work. Then she went sick on our hands. She's got no one to look after her, and we've been doing the best we can for her.'

'I see,' said Mrs Macintosh. What she thought could not be discerned. She was a woman who believed in keeping herself to herself.

A call from upstairs summoned her, and she departed, leaving Hugh to his own thoughts.

He was very distressed indeed about Mona's illness, blaming himself for it. But even if he took the whole responsibility upon himself, and he could hardly blame himself for fainting, he was distressed far beyond what he reasonably ought to be.

He heard the doctor being ushered out, and then Mrs Macintosh returned to him.

'Well?' said Hugh. 'What's the verdict?'

'A touch of bronchitis. Nothing serious in the chest. The real trouble with her is malnutrition.'

'What do you mean?'

'Miss Wilton has had no food for the last five days except the chance meals of most unsuitable things that you and Mr Jelkes have given her.'

'But, good Lord alive, what do you mean? Why hasn't she had proper meals?'

'Because, Mr Paston, the girl is out of work and starving, and you and Mr Jelkes have not had the sense to advance her any money to go on with till her wages became due, and she was too proud to ask for it.'

Hugh said nothing. There was a dead silence between them, Mrs Macintosh watching him out of inscrutable eyes. At length he said: 'Get whatever is necessary, Mrs Macintosh.'

The next few days were very boring ones for Hugh. He saw nothing of Mona, whose bronchitis was running its course, and he was of too active a nature to be content to sit indefinitely on old Jelkes' broken-down sofa and talk philosophy. He got all outstanding legal business through his hands, and then, finding himself at a loose end once more, got out the car and ran down to call on Mr Watney. The conveyancing, it seemed, was going on as well as could be expected.

'Look here,' said Mr Watney in a hushed voice, as if compounding a felony. 'You go on and take possession. You've paid your deposit. We can neither of us back out now. Miss Pumfrey isn't to know we haven't finished with the deeds.'

It was only three miles to Monks Farm, a mere step in a

car. He went round the place at his leisure, and found to his delight that what he had first taken for a second and smaller barn, proved to be a dwelling-house of much more modern structure than the rest of the buildings. Fallen plaster littered the floors; rotted window-frames let in the weather, but the main structure appeared to be sound, and he saw that it could fairly speedily be rendered habitable.

He returned to the car and sped down the road to the village at his usual gait. There Mr Huggins, the grocer, said he could recommend a builder, a really reliable man, who worked himself alongside his men. Hugh was led round behind the houses to the most amazing hugger-mugger tumble-down raffle of sheds in a cluttered yard, from which, at Mr Huggins's hail, a bearded elder appeared, who was introduced as Mr Pinker.

Yes, Mr Pinker could undertake the work – 'And glad to do so, sir. It's a shame to see a lovely bit of building like that going to rack and ruin.'

Everything being arrranged to everybody's satisfaction, Hugh went racketing off down the London road. He reached the bookshop to find Mr Jelkes and Mrs Macintosh in conclave. The abrupt break-off of the conversation at his entry told him that he must have been providing the subject-matter.

They discoursed platitudes for a few minutes, Hugh telling of his doings and his plans, and inquiring concerning Miss Wilton's progress during the few short hours he had been away.

'That's what we have been discussing,' said Jelkes. 'She's not getting on as well as she should. Her temperature still keeps up.'

'What's the cause of that?'

Jelkes looked at Mrs Macintosh. She grasped the nettle firmly. 'I think, Mr Paston, that when she saw you faint she had a far more severe shock than we realized. She has been a little light-headed, once or twice, and talked about it. She thinks you are going to do spiritualistic experiments, and she is afraid of that also. It is my belief that she is dreading meeting you again, and yet does not want to break with you because she needs the work.'

'I'm sorry. What can I do about it?'

'The best thing you can do is to go up and see her, and talk to her as if nothing had happened.'

'Hugh,' said old Jelkes, cocking a sandy eyebrow at his guest over a tea-cup, 'do you know what it is that has bitten Mona? It's Ambrosius – she's scared to death of him.'

'I've had a very strong impression of Ambrosius myself several times; but whereas I welcome it, it scares her. It's pretty strong when it comes, and if you didn't like it, as I do, I can quite believe you'd be badly scared.'

'Well, anyway, leave it alone for the present, Hugh, for the love of heaven.'

Having finished his tea, Hugh presented himself upstairs. There was no question whatever about it, she was scared of him all right. He could see it by her eyes and the way she was holding herself together. It was an extraordinary thing that Mona, who at first sight looked a very self-willed creature, was really and genuinely scared of him, and had to take her courage in both hands in order to talk to him. There was something in this that delighted Hugh profoundly, and made him esteem Mona's companionship very highly. Something that gave him the first inkling of the self-confidence he had always lacked.

'Well, how goes it?' he said.

'Not too badly,' said Mona. 'I'm much better than I was.'

'But not as well as you might be?'

'No, I'm afraid I'm not. Tiresome, isn't it?'

Silence fell between them. Hugh cast about in every direction for some remark that would prove of interest and not lead round to Ambrosius, and he could not find it. Suddenly the problem was taken out of his hands. Mona Wilton fixed her eyes on him and said: 'Have you found out anything more about Ambrosius?'

'I – I thought you did not like Ambrosius,' he said.

'I never said that,' said Mona. 'He made me feel perfectly awful because of his dreadful end, but I never said I didn't like him. As a matter of fact, I – I feel sorry for him. I think he must have had a rotten time.'

'That's exactly how I feel about him,' said Hugh. 'But you know I don't think it is very good for you to talk about Ambrosius while you're still seedy.'

'He's the best possible subject for me to talk about. I certainly shan't sleep properly till I do. Do you know what we've got to do?'

'No?'

'We've got to help him to manifest. We've got to make him welcome and bring him back. There will be no peace for anyone until we do. That's the thing I've been turning over in my mind while I've been ill. If you see Ambrosius, give him my love.' Mona smiled at him very curiously as she said the last words. There came to him a most extraordinary sense of peace and relaxation, as if something he had been straining against had given way and released him.

'I think Ambrosius really meant to be a reformer, given half a chance. He wasn't just abreacting his complexes by playing with dirt. He knew, whatever they liked to say, that Pan was clean and natural.'

There flashed before Mona's memory the expression on the sharp-featured face of the stranger who had bent over her in the empty upper room of the museum, and she wondered what chains upon the soul Ambrosius would have to break before he reached the relative freedom indicated by Hugh Paston's viewpoint. A sudden pang of fear shook her; for although she did not fear Pan, she feared, and not without reason, the overwhelming rush when barriers go down.

'If our hypothesis is right,' Hugh went on, 'Ambrosius was trying to raise Pan.'

'And Pan,' said Mona eagerly, 'is elemental force. He comes up from the earth under your feet, just as spiritual force, the sun-force, comes down from the sky over your head.'

The door opened, and Mrs Macintosh entered.

'I think she has talked enough for one visit,' said the housekeeper, and Hugh went like a lamb.

Left alone, Mona dropped back on the pillows and

clasped her hands behind her head. Hugh liked her, that was obvious; he seemed to want her with him all the time; he referred everything to her. But all the same, he did not give her the impression of being attracted to her as a woman. Old Jelkes had taught her a good deal of the secret knowledge on the subject of sex that is so important a part of the Mystery Tradition – one of its secret keys, in fact. She knew that there must be some degree of reaction between a man and a woman whenever any appreciable degree of sympathetic relationship is established between them, but she did not make the mistake of thinking it need be crudely sexual. She knew the subtle interplay of magnetism that goes on all the time in every relationship between the more vital and positive of the pair and the more pliant and dependent, quite irrespective of sex. She knew that, so far as magnetism went, in her relationship with Hugh Paston she was far the more positive of the pair. Hugh was peculiarly negative; peculiarly lacking in any sort of magnetism.

But then there was Ambrosius, who was a very different matter. But who, or what, was Ambrosius? First of all, he could be the dissociated personality of Hugh himself. Secondly, he might be the spirit of the dead monk manifesting through Hugh, who was quite negative enough for any sort of mediumship. Or thirdly, the explanation might lie in the far-reaching doctrine of reincarnation.

The negative, purposeless, gentle-natured Hugh might be putty in anybody's hands, but Ambrosius was another matter. He promised to be a very awkward handful, whether he were a dissociated personality or a separate entity. Mona did not know what to do with him because she could not be sure exactly what he was. How could one tell a dissociated personality from a spirit-control, and a spirit-control from a previous incarnation of the same person? Anyway, the practical results were the same, whatever theory might be chosen to explain them.

At that moment the door opened and in walked Jelkes. 'Where's Hugh?' he exclaimed in surprise, finding Mona alone.

'I've no idea. Mrs Macintosh turfed him out some time

ago. Good Lord, did you think he was spending the night with me?'

'Mona, I wish you wouldn't talk like that. I don't like to hear it.'

'Don't take any notice of me, Uncle Jelkes, my bark is a lot worse than my bite. You ought to know that by this time.' She hesitated for a moment and then said: 'Uncle, what is Ambrosius really, do you think?'

'That's exactly what I have been addling my brains over, Mona. If it's mediumship, there will be the devil to pay. He's in no state to stand it. The kind of mediumship that develops under strain is always pathological, in my opinion. I think it's a dual personality, myself.'

'I believe that Hugh was Ambrosius in his last incarnation, and what we know as Hugh today, all nerves and inhibitions, is what was left of Ambrosius after the Pope's visitor had finished with him. Then, when he invoked Pan, he opened up his own subconscious, which is what Pan always does, and the first thing he struck was the layer of memories belonging to Ambrosius, all full of emotion because Ambrosius died a terrible death. It's a psycho-pathology all right; it's a dual personality all right – two men under one hat, but it doesn't start in this incarnation, it goes back to the last.'

Jelkes sat for a long time deep in thought. At length he spoke. 'I believe you're right, Mona. That explains a lot of things that fit in with each other.'

Jelkes knew that in tackling the problem in psycho-pathology presented by Hugh Paston he was taking on a very nasty job – particularly nasty, because the girl was inevitably involved in it. Rouse the Pan Within, and he makes contact with the Great God, the First-begotten Love. Mona Wilton had caused a reflex stir of the instincts in Hugh Paston, whether he knew it or not. If Mona chose to follow up her advantage, the invocation of Pan would be an unqualified success. It was a tricky business. There would be a sudden rush of repressed emotion, like the bursting of a mill-dam, and then Hugh would rapidly come back to normal; and once back to normal, it was exceedingly unlikely that he would have any use for Mona Wilton.

86

If he could be sure that Mona would keep her head, and neither panic at the manifestation, nor get her personal feelings involved, the way to handle Hugh was deliberately to wake the Inner Pan till it burst its inhibitions and the two sides of Hugh's nature joined up. And Jelkes knew how it could be done. Steadily, deliberately, under control all the time, as the ancient priests did it – by means of ritual. But it was Mona who would have to do it. He had no word of power that would evoke Pan to visible appearance in the soul of Hugh Paston. It is one thing to tackle a nasty job oneself; but it is quite another to put someone else on to do it.

Mona's voice interrupted his thoughts. 'Do you know what I believe is the only solution of Mr Paston's problems? Do a ceremony of invocation and bring Pan through. You will have him under control then.'

'That's just what I was thinking myself, Mona. But if we do that, who's going to do the invocation? I can't. Pan won't come for me.'

'Me, I suppose,' said Mona. 'Lord, what a life! I never thought I'd come to this. But it is the only thing that will straighten things out. He will go on the rocks if we can't do something for him.'

'I'd like to help him, Mona, but what you're proposing is no joke, and you're the person who is going to have to stand the brunt of it. You'll have to lead him up the garden path, and then nip from under at the critical moment.'

Hugh would have liked to have said good-bye to Miss Wilton before he took his departure next morning, but this Mrs Macintosh would not permit, alleging that the doctor was expected. He was vouchsafed the information, however, that Miss Wilton had had a good night, and was much better this morning. Although her prescription had worked well, Mrs Macintosh had no intention of risking an overdose.

A bedlam of noise greeted Hugh as he approached the farm, and he discovered that Mr Pinker had been as good as his word, and the place looked as if it had been bombed. All the raffle of unsightly shacks in the courtyard was piled in a heap in the centre, giving promise of a noble bonfire. Even as he crossed the muddy expanse, a couple of youths came out of a doorway laden with dilapidated planks to which the garish remains of flowered wallpapers still clung. Things were moving.

It was now possible to see the fan-arching and the delicate pillars of the cloisters surrounding the four sides of the yard. To the east there were no buildings backing on to the cloisters, and the grove of Scotch firs overhung them with their branches and dropped cones and needles on to the lichened stone of their roof. To the north they were overshadowed by the steep-pitched roof of the chapel. To the south, the dwelling-house backed on to them; to the west, the main building of the ancient priory.

He entered the main building by a big door that stood wide open, and found that the last of the partitioning lay on the floor and it was possible to get a view of the big rooms. They lay one either side of the large hall with its groined roof and fine curving stone stair. The whole place appeared to be built of stone, the only timber being the doors. Hugh thought of the cold during the long winters, and the imprisoned monks in their unheated cells; there were big stone fireplaces in the two large rooms, but he doubted if the prisoners got much benefit from them.

And yet the place did not seem melancholy to him. It was as if the terrible happenings that marked the close of its ecclesiastical career had been swept away and it was back at the days of its building, when its master, full of new hope, got his risky enterprise going.

Hugh walked round his domain. The labourers were busy smashing out the rough woodwork that defaced the older portion of the building, but in the dwelling-house the skilled men were at work on the repairs. Old Pinker himself was busy with the window-frames.

'You do want to make a place weather-tight before you does aught else,' said he as Hugh greeted him.

Having arrived at Thorley, Hugh did not keep on running backwards and forwards to Billings Street, as he had planned to do. Things were happening inside him that made him think, and made him wish to be alone while he thought.

He was very puzzled as to exactly what had happened in

the upper room at the museum, where he was supposed to have fainted. But had he fainted? The last thing he heard before he lost consciousness had been the great bell of the Abbey striking the hour, and he had recovered consciousness to hear the chiming of the quarter. He had been sitting down when he had lost consciousness, and he had been flat on his back on the floor, well clear of any chair, when he recovered it. It does not take a man a quarter of an hour to fall from horizontal to vertical when he faints. Moreover, there had been a marked change in Mona Wilton's attitude towards him from that moment; she had registered fear in no mistakable manner. Jelkes, too, had cooled off appreciably.

The one thing he had to hold on to was Mona's curious remark: 'We must help Ambrosius to come through. Give him my love', and the extraordinary lifting of the cloud that had followed her words. There came to his mind the idea that the disincarnate Ambrosius might have turned up and made use of him as a medium. The idea left him cold, however. It would not in the least amuse him to be a trance medium. An overwhelming rush of sympathy, for Ambrosius was the last thing he remembered before losing consciousness. It seemed to him that he had realized so clearly what Ambrosius was trying to do and how he must have felt, that for a moment he had actually identified himself with the dead monk.

When Mona laid her hand on his wrist, he had reacted as Ambrosius would have reacted. He had experienced the tremendous upheaval that might have been expected to take place in the soul of the monk, totally unaccustomed to women, who had secretly broken with his religion and all its inhibitions, and was pursuing the cult of Pan.

It was a bewildering problem, and Hugh, sitting over the fire in the stuffy little parlour at the Green Man, gave himself up to the contemplation of it.

And as he did so, he felt the same change coming over him again. And for a brief moment he *was* Ambrosius. And he felt the tremendous concentration of will and energy, the daring, and at the same time the subtlety and wariness, that had characterized the renegade monk. Once again he was adrift in time and space and was afraid. But at the same time he felt a strange exhilaration and sense of flowing power.

This was a most extraordinary thing. Here was he, the living image of the dead monk with whom he felt such a profound sympathy and whose house he had got! What did it all mean? He rose, pulled on his leather coat, went and fetched the car from the shed that housed it, and sped down the long mile to Monks Farm.

There was no one there when he arrived, Mr Pinker having called his men off to give first aid to a cowshed that threatened to fall down upon its occupants. The first faint dusk was gathering as Hugh made his way round the buildings, and using his duplicate key, he let himself into what had once been the large chapel of the priory.

The rough boarding at the west end had been taken down, and revealed the skeleton of a stone-mullioned rose-window of lovely proportions, with fragments of stained glass still clinging here and there in the highest angles. The dirt floor had been dug out, and revealed patterned tiles. In a corner under the window, carefully laid on an old sack, was a pile of bits of broken, multicoloured glass, that had evidently been picked out of the dirt of the floor as it was shovelled away. Hugh was delighted. He would have a fascinating time piecing the bits together like a jigsaw puzzle and having them restored to their place in the tracery.

Standing beneath the west window, through which the last of the light struck upwards from the sunset, he saw that the roof was steep-pitched, and very lofty for the size of the building, and that it was divided into five bays by buttress pillars. In each bay he could just discern the dim lines of a vast winged figure, evidently an angel.

The east end, contrary to the custom of churches, presented a blank wall instead of a window, and upon its great height Hugh could see the shadowy outlines of a painting. He walked slowly up the aisle, and as he advanced, the picture became clearer, and he saw that it represented a vast green tree bearing multi-coloured fruit. Ten of them, he counted, in the faded remains of crude primary colours, arranged in stiff triangles, three by three, with the odd one low down on the trunk at the bottom.

Immediately in the centre, as if it were a pot for the tree to grow in, was a square stone pedestal like a short pillar, waist-high. Hugh wondered what in the world this had been, for it was exactly where the altar ought to have stood. On the stonework of the wall he could see clearly the marks where the altar had been fastened, and it evidently completely enclosed the stone pedestal.

Three steps led up from the nave of the chapel into the sanctuary, and there the tiling ended and mosaic began. He saw that the design on the mosaic represented the twelve signs of the Zodiac, with the seven planets within their circle, and the symbols of the four elements of earth, air, fire and water in the centre. It was an exact reproduction of a picture in one of Jelkes' books.

Then the solution of the curious stone pedestal, enclosed in the altar, suddenly dawned on him. He had been reading about exactly the same thing in another of Jelkes' books. One of the charges against the Knights Templars was that they had made cubical stone altars to the goat-god, Baphomet, and concealed them underneath orthodox wooden table-altars, made to open up like cupboard doors, so that the unitiated suspected nothing.

Hugh was thrilled to the marrow. This chapel, outwardly Christian, was inwardly pagan. No wonder they bricked up Ambrosius!

It was fast becoming too dark to see any details of the shadowy building, and as he sat, he felt a curious sensation. It seemed to him as if the chapel were the focus of all the forces of the universe and they all converged upon it. He sat listening, as it were, to the sensation, and it went on steadily, like the sound of a waterfall. The chapel grew darker and darker, and he rose, groped his way round the buildings, switched on the car headlights with a sense of relief, and returned to the Green Man.

Settling down over the fire after his meal with a cup of tea and a cigarette Hugh set to work to puzzle out the situation concerning Mona Wilton, whom at first sight he had not found to be particularly prepossessing, but who was gradually becoming – he did not quite know what. A friend, unquestionably, but that was an odd relationship to have with a youngish woman.

Hugh was accustomed to women who took love-making as a matter of course, but Mona obviously did not want him to flirt with her, in fact, would have strongly objected to any attempt at so doing. He also suspected that even as a friend, she intended to keep him at arm's length. In one way he liked the unacknowledged friendship, with its steady sense of fidelity and goodwill, better than any more explicit and open relationship, which might have proved embarrassing; but on the other hand, the manhood in him wanted to press on to more intimate matters. It slowly dawned on him that he was getting awfully fond of her. Not in love with her, as he had been with his wife, who had been a very beautiful and very sensual woman, but just fond of her. He couldn't describe it in any other way, even to himself. Mona Wilton was very far from being a sensual woman. She treated him like a brother, and nothing more. Hugh was so used to that deep, inner, spiritual loneliness of the soul which lies so heavily upon those who live in an unsympathetic environment, that he had accepted it as the natural lot of man, never having known anything else. The lines he had read as a schoolboy stuck in his head when all the Imagists were forgotten –

> '*Yes, in the sea of life enisled,*
> *With echoing straits between us thrown,*
> *Dotting the shoreless, water wild,*
> *We million mortals live alone.*'

These seemed to him, even when he read them first, to enshrine an ineluctable truth, and life had confirmed it. Hugh felt more acutely than ever that the only thing he had to offer anybody was his money, and if they did not want that – what had he to give them? He went to bed very depressed; lay on his back and tried to dream of Greece, but only succeeded in dreaming of his mother, who seemed to be angry with him.

Mr Pinker, under the stimulus of Hugh's constant presence, bestirred himself in a way he might not have done if left to his own devices, and the smaller house was fast approaching habitability. Hugh dropped Mrs Macintosh a line requesting her presence, and that lady duly turned up in the local taxi, dressed in impeccable housekeeper's black, as was her invariable custom. She had entirely recovered her poise, and expressed neither approval nor disapproval when Hugh introduced her to the farm, but merely acquiesced. She measured and took notes as bidden, and finally, equally professionally, took her seat in Hugh's unhandy racing car and permitted him to run her down to the station.

As they waited on the platform for the train, she said to him: 'How much longer do you think you will want me, Mr Paston?'

'I was wondering whether you would care to take charge at the farm?'

'No,' said Mrs Macintosh emphatically, 'I would not. It feels sinister to me. Sinister and wicked. I don't know how you can stand it. I wouldn't live there for anything you could offer me.'

Hugh, who had not counted on Highland psychism backed by Highland Calvinism, was nonplussed. His plans were going astray. How was he going to get Mona Wilton to come to the farm unless Mrs Macintosh were there to play propriety and look after her while she was still convalescent?

'I think I ought to tell you, Mr Paston, that Lady Paston came to the bookshop to inquire after you, and Mr Jelkes was very short with her. She is very anxious about you, and I do not think that Mr Jelkes' attitude allayed her anxiety.'

Hugh groaned. 'Does she know about the farm?'

'She knows nothing. Mr Jelkes refused to tell her a thing, and was, if you will pardon my saying so, very rude to her. Miss Wilton and I sat in the kitchenette with the light out while she was there.'

'Why ever did you do that?'

'I thought the position of Miss Wilton might be misunderstood, and involve you in unpleasantness.'

'I don't see why. Oh, well, no good worrying about that. Here is your train.'

'Thank you very much, Mr Paston. And if it is convenient to you, I would like to get off at the end of the week. I have the offer of another post, and I want to pay a visit to some friends in Scotland before accepting it. I do not think Miss Wilton needs me any longer.'

Hugh put her into the train with a sigh of relief. She was a good woman. She was a kind woman. She was trustworthy. She was efficient. He liked and respected her, but one could not associate Mrs Macintosh with attendance at a rite of Pan.

Knowing that she meant to go North, and that she had a long journey before her, he thought he would be quite safe in putting in an appearance at the bookshop round about lunch-time on Saturday. Arriving at the bookshop, he found to his surprise that Mrs Macintosh was still there.

'Might I have a word with you, Mr Paston?' she said. 'I wish to apologize for the way I spoke of your new house. And I hope, I hope very much, that I have not put you to inconvenience if you were counting on me to look after it for you, but I couldn't – I really couldn't go there, Mr Paston. You know, we have second sight in our family, and I am certain I should see things.'

'Did you see anything there?'

Mrs Macintosh flinched. She would not tell a lie, and she did not want to tell the truth. Such people are at a great disadvantage. 'It was your face, Mr Paston.'

'My face? What do you mean?'

'Your face changed completely as you went into the old part of the house.' She looked at him sharply. 'Did you know that?'

The tables were turned on Hugh, and he too had either to lie or give information he had no mind to. For as he had crossed the threshold he had thought of Ambrosius, and for a brief second the curious sensation had come to him that he sometimes got when he thought of the renegade monk.

'I think it must have been this that Miss Wilton spoke of when she was light-headed one night,' continued Mrs

94

Macintosh. 'I could not think at the time why it had frightened her so badly, but I understood as soon as I saw it. It is very alarming, Mr Paston, I don't think you quite realize how you look when you do that.'

'But look here, Mrs Macintosh, you've been with us over two years, and I've never done anything desperate that I know of, why are you suddenly getting scared of me now?'

'I am not scared of you, Mr Paston.' Mrs Macintosh bridled indignantly at this aspersion. 'But when you change before my very eyes into somebody else – I think you will admit that is enough to alarm anybody.'

'You think that was what scared Miss Wilton?'

'Yes, I'm certain it was. You seemed to get into her dreams when her temperature was up, and she called out in her sleep, not once but several times, "Don't turn into Ambrosius again—!" She was badly frightened, Mr Paston; and I don't mind telling you, so was I when I saw you do it.'

Before he could reply a battery of knocks sounded on the shop door. 'Excuse me,' said Mrs Macintosh, 'I expect that is the man for my luggage,' and she went down the narrow, dusty stairs. Hugh heard her open the door at the bottom and an exclamation of surprise followed.

'Mrs Macintosh, *you* here?' he heard in the voice of his eldest sister.

'Yes, Lady Whitney,' came the noncommittal tones of the Scotswoman.

'I want to see my brother. His car is outside, so it is no use saying he isn't here.'

Hugh thought that the best thing to do was to bow to the inevitable. He did not want Alice to have a stand-up row with old Jelkes. Knowing them both, he thought they would come to blows.

He came down the stairs. 'Hullo, Alice?' he said.

'So there you are, Hugh? We have been looking for you everywhere. Whatever is the meaning of all this nonsense?'

'Well, I thought I would like to get away from everything and be quiet for a bit.'

'You might have let us know where you were. It has been

most inconvenient. Everybody asking, and no letters answered. Where were you, all this time?'

'Never mind where. I'd sooner not tell you. Just a place of retreat that I want to keep quiet.'

'By yourself?'

'Yes, of course.'

'Then who is this Miss Wilton?'

'She's an artist I've been employing to do the decorations for my new house.'

'Where?'

'That's not your business.'

'What has come over you? I've never known you like this before. What's all this secrecy about?'

'The secrecy is because I don't want to be bothered. That's all there is to it.'

'Do you expect me to believe that?'

'I don't care whether you believe it or not.'

A tide of anger utterly unlike anything he had ever known before, had been rising in Hugh while they were wrangling, and suddenly it brimmed over in a flood of rage that held him speechless. A curious heat and burning went through him, and he found himself staring down into the face of a strange woman whose flushed angry cheeks gradually went dead white under her paint. He pointed to the door and said 'Get out!' and she went without another word.

He walked up the stairs again and at the top saw another strange woman, and heard her calling to someone in a terrified voice. The place was unfamiliar, he did not know where he was. A man came, and behind him yet another woman, peering anxiously round his shoulder. And he knew that woman!

For the first time he saw in the flesh the face he had so often seen in his dreams. The succuba that had haunted his sleep for years. Now he saw her. And he could not take his eyes off her, nor could she take hers off him.

He knew the risk; and yet he felt that nothing mattered compared to that one thing, and that at all costs he must grasp it lest it slipped out of his reach for ever. He stepped

96

forward, put the man aside, and gripped the woman by the arm, drawing her towards him. He looked down into her eyes. Greenish eyes, as one would expect in a succuba; but he realized instantly that this was no evil demon sent to lead men's souls astray. The eyes were steady and sincere, and looked straight back into his. The eyes of a woman, not a fiend.

And he realized with a dreadful hopelessness his isolation; the bondage of his vows; his powerlessness to escape from the life to which he had been given before he knew life's meaning. He was cut off from all this. He must let go of this woman or he would ruin himself. And then something fierce and terrible rose up in him and said that he might ruin himself, but he would not let go of her.

A sound behind him made him turn round, and there stood the woman he had already driven off, and with her another and older woman who looked like her mother. They spoke to him, but their dialect was incomprehensible save for a word here and there. His wits had returned to him, however, and with them, his dignity. He put the succuba behind him, though he still kept tight hold of her, and saluted them gravely, as became a churchman of his standing. He could see that they were non-plussed. The old man then took a hand and talked with them animatedly in their dialect, of which Hugh understood enough to gather that some learned person was to be summoned forthwith. They departed, plainly very angry and upset, and the old man took him by the shoulders and said:

'Hugh, you damn fool, you stop this nonsense or I'll punch your head!'

A sudden giddiness passed over him. He felt himself sway, and if someone had not caught him, would have fallen. Then he recovered himself, and found Jelkes and Mrs Macintosh confronting him with consternation written all over their faces.

'Hullo?' he said, feeling very foolish. 'Have I been having one of my seizures? I suppose this is what you have been complaining of?' turning to Mrs Macintosh.

'Yes, Mr Paston, that is exactly it,' was the reply. 'And if you would let go of Miss Wilton, I think she'd be relieved.'

Hugh turned round startled, to find Mona behind him.

'What's it all about?' he demanded.

'That's what we'd like to know,' said Jelkes, grimly. He led the way down into the shop, and they all followed. Hugh felt he had never been so glad to see anything in his life as he was to see the warmth and cosiness of the little back parlour. It seemed to him as if he had just come out of a long and vivid nightmare of cold, and stone walls, and loneliness, and frustration.

'How are you feeling, Hugh?' said the old bookseller, turning to him abruptly.

'All right. A bit shaken. What happened?'

'Goodness only knows. A change of consciousness of some sort. But they've gone to fetch the doctor, and if you don't watch your step, they'll get you certified. For the love of God, Hugh, keep your hair on when the doctor comes.'

'So that's the game, is it?' said Hugh. 'That's a new one. They've tried a good many things, but they've never tried that before. Tell me frankly, Jelkes, is there any likelihood of their being able to do it?'

'Well, laddie, frankly, there is, if they give their minds to it. Not that you need certifying, or anything like it, but you've got bones that are worth picking, Hugh, and that's what has always been your trouble.'

A resounding bang at the door startled them. Jelkes girt his dressing-gown about him with a determined air, and went striding off through the bookshop, murder in his eye. He returned in a moment, crestfallen.

'It's the man for your box,' he said to Mrs Macintosh, and together they departed upstairs, leaving Hugh alone with Mona.

He sat down on the sofa, facing her. 'I know that certification game. I've seen it played before. Tell me frankly, was what happened just now the same as what happened in the museum?'

'Yes.'

'That was what scared you into your illness, wasn't it?'

'Yes, I'm afraid it was.'

'I'd be truly thankful to understand all this. Tell me, Mona, tell me all you can.'

'I'd sooner Uncle Jelkes told you. Wait till he comes back from seeing Mrs Macintosh off.'

'Is she going? I must say good-bye to her.'

He rose from the sofa, but a sudden sound of altercation in the front shop made Mona catch his hand and pull him back. Uncle Jelkes was evidently denying admission to someone who was demanding it with authority. Jelkes settled the argument by telling him to go to hell and slamming the door with such force that all the books in the window fell down. After that there was silence.

'I've been busy at the farm,' said Hugh. I've got it pretty nearly straight now. Let's all pack up and go down there. We'll shunt the whole party and leave no trail. We'll be hard to trace if we get off promptly. They haven't sold my big Rolls yet. She's sitting at the garage. I'll run the sports car back and get the other.'

'I will if Uncle will,' she said.

At that moment Jelkes reappeared. 'Mrs Macintosh got off all right,' he said. 'Asked me to say good-bye to you for her.'

'Sorry to have missed her,' said Hugh. 'She was a good sort, but a trifle oppressive. I don't believe she'd have fitted in with Pan.'

'Hugh's got a suggestion to make, Uncle Jelkes,' said Mona.

Hugh outlined the plan, and Jelkes looked at Mona.

'That's what we're going to do, Uncle Jelkes,' said she quietly. 'It's the only thing to do. We shall have all sorts of trouble if Hugh stops here.'

'Yes,' said Jelkes, 'I know we shall. But, Lord, I wish it wasn't the farm!'

'It's got to be the farm, Uncle Jelkes. There's nothing to do but grip the nettle. You know that as well as I do.'

'Magnificent,' cried Hugh, leaping to his feet. 'You two sling a few things together, and I'll go and get the car,' and he vanished before they had time to change their minds.

CHAPTER SIX

Hugh slammed the big Rolls-Royce through the traffic, and as they reached the open road the great headlights went on and the car settled down to her beautiful gait, eating up the miles until it slid silent as a ghost across the common and down the lane to the farm. Hugh pulled up beside the dark and silent buildings, switched on the inside light, and turned in the driving-seat to speak to his companions.

There, in his corner, sat Jelkes, looking like an old cock gone broody, with Mona asleep on his shoulder. The sight affected Hugh in an indescribable manner. It seemed to him that the deepest springs in his nature would be fed if a woman did that to him. Mona woke up and raised her head and their eyes met. Hugh turned away hastily lest his face should say too much.

'Well, we get out here,' he said. He opened the car door and held out his hand to help Mona to alight. 'Come on. I know it's like burgling a tomb at the moment, but we'll soon have it more cheerful.'

They entered, the air striking cold and dank and smelling of fresh plaster. Hugh, who had no matches, struck a light on his pocket lighter, and held up the dim blue flame to illuminate their surroundings. They were not too bad. The reproduction furniture that Hugh had installed was inoffensive and went well enough with the old farm-house. Hugh lit a battered hurricane lamp hanging from a beam, and the place began to look more like a human habitation and less like the family vault.

'Now for a fire,' said Hugh.

Jelkes followed him through a door that led into a scullery, and thence into what had been the farmyard, and there, in the centre, they saw dimly in the moonlight an enormous pile of old lumber. They each gathered up an armful, returned to the living-room, and deposited their loads in the great empty fire-place. Hugh went out to the car and returned with a grease-gun and shot black oil all over the pile. He touched a match to it, and it went up like a volcano.

'Now then, T.J., I'll leave you to stoke. I'm going to the village to get some supplies.'

Arriving at the village, he was faced by the delicate task of breaking it to Mrs Pascoe, the landlady of the Green Man pub, that he was about to desert her. Things were not made any easier, however, by the fact that she apparently had company in her sanctum behind the bar, for someone was singing a languorous and long-drawn-out ditty to the accompaniment of an accordion in there. However, there was nothing for it, and Hugh overcame his shyness and knocked on the door. The accordion died away with a wail like a despairing tom-cat, the door opened, and a man stood there, obviously a seaman of the roughest type.

'Hullo?' said Hugh, too taken aback to think of anything else.

'Hullo yerself,' said the stranger, 'and what might you be wantin'?'

'I wanted a word with Mrs Pascoe,' said Hugh.

'She's gone across to the shop. Back in a minute. I'm her son. Come inside and sit down,' and ushered him into the lamp-lit, smoke-clouded, low-ceilinged snuggery.

' 'Ave one with me?' he said, taking up a stone jug that stood on the table amid the remains of a meal.

'I don't mind if I do,' said Hugh, 'I've had no lunch.'

'Bite of supper?' said the seaman.

'No, I won't do that,' said Hugh. 'I've got some people waiting for me, and I want to get some supper for them too; that's what I want to see Mrs Pascoe about.'

'She'll be back in two tweaks. Where are you from?'

'Up at Monks Farm.'

'Ah, so you're Mr Paston. Ma wasn't expecting you back till Monday.'

A bumping in the passage announced the return of Mrs Pascoe, her arms full of parcels. Hugh explained his predicament. He had an old gentleman and a young lady, his niece, Hugh added hastily, up at the farm, and the young lady was only just out of bed, having been ill.

Mrs Pascoe was horrified, and flew round like a hen in a corn-bin. Hugh was immensely amused to see what was her notion of the primary necessities of life. A case of bottled beer, two bottles of port and a bottle of whisky made their way into the car almost of their own volition. Then at his suggestion, she got in too. Without waiting for any suggestion her nautical offspring added himself to the party, and they set off in the Rolls-Royce for Mr Huggins, the grocer.

They formed a human chain, with Mr Huggins and Mrs Pascoe at the business end and himself and Bill as mindless links in outer darkness beside the car, and it seemed as if the entire contents of the shop were being passed out to them. In fact, it was only Bill's scientific stowage that enabled the Rolls to hold the stuff. Finally Mrs Pascoe and Mr Huggins came out to supervise the last of the loading and to wave good-bye as Hugh drove the heavily laden Rolls away.

Firelight shone out of the farm windows so brightly that Hugh wondered whether it had caught alight. But no, Jelkes had merely done as instructed, and stoked efficiently. A furnace roared up the chimney, throwing more light than the lamp.

Mona, her toes on the hearth, looked much more like herself than she had done for a long time. He drew a chair up to the hearth beside her, and dropped into it. 'Mona, I want to talk to you. Old Jelkes cannot stay on here forever – after all, he has a business to run.' He hesitated for a moment, and then went on: 'You know Mrs Macintosh has let me down?'

'Yes, so she told us. I think she was right, you know. It wouldn't have worked.'

Hugh nodded. 'I know, but it does present a problem. Look, Mrs Pascoe has been telling me about a really good servant girl that she could get for us. If this girl comes to live with us here at the farm will you stop on after Uncle Jelkes goes home?'

Mona thought for a minute. 'I don't see why I shouldn't,' she said at length. Her Bohemian soul cared nothing for the unconventionality of the situation. There had been a momentary flutter of fear at the thought of coping with Ambrosius single-handed after Jelkes had left, but she steeled her heart. After all, what prospects had she beyond her job with Hugh?

Mona was the first to awake next morning, Hugh and Mr Jelkes being constitutionally late risers. She looked out of her window and saw the first young green on the birches, and the first sunlight over the firs, and as soon as might be she was out of doors. Living in London so long, she had hardly realized what the spring and the morning could mean to her. Some polyanthuses, velvet-brown and wine-purple, had joined the daffodils in the coarse grass at the foot of the old wall, and Mona, made sensitive by her illness, stood and looked at them. Dew sparkled on every grey blade of the dry winter grass, the heavy dew left behind by late frosts, and the little velvety faces of the polyanthuses looked up through it unharmed. The sky was the pale blue of early spring and early morning; a little mare's tail of clouds to the south showed the way of the wind, which came in soft breaths, blowing away the chill of the dawn. Dark gorse with yellow bloom dotted the unthrifty pasture, silver birches rising among it made a fine lace of twigs against the sky, shot through as the light caught them with a faint haze of new green. The dark firs stood against the skyline as they had stood the year through, unchanging. Against the winter grey of the pasture broad stretches of bracken lay tawny; unfenced, the field stretched away and dropped into a wood with the fall of the ground. The sylvan Pan held his own here, and gave no inch to Ceres.

A hand through her arm made her jump nearly out of her skin, and she turned round to see Hugh looking down on her from his ungainly height. He smiled, and gave her arm a squeeze. 'Lovely, isn't it?' he said.

'Very lovely,' said Mona, and they stood together silently.

A clop-clop on the drive attracted their attention, and they saw Mr Pinker arriving in an old-fashioned gig with a most extraordinary load on board, which included Mrs Pascoe, Bill Pascoe, the foreman, a boy, a quantity of planks, and in Mrs Pascoe's motherly arms a steaming glue-pot.

Jelkes, who had left his dressing-gown behind out of politeness, ambled down in his Inverness cape and lent a touch of picturesqueness to the assemblage. Mona, whose neutral-tinted clothes seemed so drab in London, looked here as if she had risen from the grey winter pasture like Aphrodite from the foam of the sea, so perfectly did she match her surroundings.

They set the door of the living-room wide open and carried the table into the patch of sunshine that came streaming in. Mona picked some of the polyanthus and set them in a rough little earthenware jar she found on a shelf in the scullery, and placed them on the table among the gay cottage crockery, and a bee came bumbling in and got the honey from them. Hugh suddenly realized that there was a kind of happiness that had almost the quality of inebriation.

It was a great joy to them both to show Jelkes all there was to see of the interesting old buildings. Jelkes, for his part, was amused to observe that Mona was quite as possessive as Hugh in her attitude towards them.

Mona had not seen them since the general clearance of partitions and other impedimenta had taken place, and she was now able for the first time to appreciate the possibilities of the two beautiful big rooms with their fan-arching and fine fire-places. Ambrosius had evidently been a gentleman of taste who had done himself well – within the limits of ecclesiastical architectural conventions.

Returned to the dwelling-house, they were confronted by Mrs Pascoe, who had rallied all her forces with a view to planting upon them the prize skivvy, whom she was determined they should have. It appeared that there were wheels within wheels in this matter, and it gradually transpired that Miss Pumfrey was in the habit of running her establishment with the help of girls from 'Homes'. In varying periods of time, however, these unhappy fledglings became full-fledged, realized how they were being imposed upon, and gave in their notice. Consequently they had to be replaced. Miss Pumfrey, therefore, ran her establishment with a steady succession of ignorant orphans, which the village took a malicious delight in educating in the ways of the world, for Miss Pumfrey was not popular.

The latest orphan, however, had stuck. She had been with Miss Pumfrey over a year, and in all this time she had never been out alone, but always in the company of either the elderly parlour-maid or Miss Pumfrey herself. According to Mrs Pascoe the girl was a deserving girl, being imposed upon, who wanted to better herself. After she had withdrawn, the three of them looked at each other.

'If you take that girl, you've made an enemy for life of Miss Pumfrey,' said Jelkes.

'Do you know,' said Mona, 'I don't think I've ever met anyone I've disliked quite as much as Miss Pumfrey. I'd love to snitch her skivvy.'

Mona went to tell Mrs Pascoe they would have the girl, and see what arrangements could be made for her transference, to learn that arrangements had already been made, and the girl was waiting to be fetched, and Hugh drove off with Mrs Pascoe in the Rolls forthwith.

Left alone, Jelkes cocked a sandy eyebrow at his ewe-lamb, and said: 'Well, Mona, what are you brewing?'

'I had been going to tell you, Uncle, only I haven't had the chance. Mr Paston was talking to me just before you came down, and he suggested that if I had this girl with me, I could stop on here after you had gone back. It would be far handier like that while I am getting the place shipshape.'

Jelkes sat in thought for a few minutes. 'Well, Mona,' he said at length. 'It's your funeral.'

'Are you against it, Uncle?'

'I don't know what to say. I don't see what other alternative you've got. I suppose, providing you keep your head and handle things shrewdly, you'll be all right, but I can't say I'm happy about Ambrosius, and the girl would be no protection to you. Look here, why don't you work up a job for Bill here? He's been sounding me about it. He'd be very useful as handy-man, gardener, and general roustabout. I'd be happy, at least, much happier, about you, if you had Bill around.'

'You do amuse me, Uncle, proposing a regular cut-throat like Bill as protection from Hugh, who's the mildest of souls.'

'Not so damn mild, Mona. And anyway, the milder Hugh is, the bigger handful Ambrosius will be.'

'It strikes me that one would obtain an awfully nice result if Hugh and Ambrosius were melted and mixed into one man.'

'That is exactly what wants doing, but how it is to be done is more than I know. We'll just sit tight for a fortnight and see how things pan out.'

'What are you scared of, Uncle?'

'I'm scared of two things, child. Ambrosius is either a previous incarnation of Hugh's or a split personality. For all practical purposes it doesn't matter which. Everything that's shut down in Hugh is in Ambrosius – unchecked. Hugh is pecking his way out of his shell, and as he comes out, Ambrosius is coming out too – with a rush. If you don't handle Ambrosius just right, there'll be the devil to pay.'

Meanwhile Hugh was waiting in the car in the village for Mrs Pascoe and the servant girl. Finally they came staggering along with a tin trunk between them. Hugh wondered what might be the reason for all this secrecy. Surely the girl could walk out at any moment provided she did not mind abandoning the wages due to her. But the moment they came alongside, he knew. He had only to take one look at the pair of vague brown eyes gazing up from that moon-like face to know the kind of Home that Miss Pumfrey, in despair, had got her latest servant from. He wondered what were the penalties for kidnapping idiot orphans, and his heart sank into his boots.

But it was too late to back out now. Mrs Pascoe hurled the trunk into the car, hurled the girl in after it, and then scrambled in herself. Hugh sighed, and drove back to the farm by a devious route, as instructed.

Leaving Mrs Pascoe and her protégée to dispose of the tin trunk, he stalked into the living-room and announced: 'Mona, she's loopy!'

Mona leapt to her feet. 'What, my new skivvy?'

'Serve you jolly well right, the pair of you,' said Jelkes. A knocking at the door caused Hugh to stand aside and open it, and there was Mrs Pascoe.

'Now it's all right, Mr Paston, sir, you've nothing to trouble about. I see'd by your face what you felt. I know she comes from the Silly Home, but you've nothing to worry about. Them sort make the best kind of servants provided you get 'em with just the right amount of silliness. They do as they're bid.'

'I see,' said Hugh, who was in internal fits at the débâcle, and the faces of Mona and Mrs Pascoe. 'Well, you'd better settle it between you,' he said, and headed for the door, feeling he would disgrace himself if he stopped a moment longer. He was followed equally precipitately by Jelkes. Safely out in the yard, they leant up against the wall and exploded. Bill sauntered up.

' 'Ullo?' he said. 'Has Ma stuck you with Silly Lizzie?' and joined shamelessly in the laughter.

Presently Mona joined them. 'You're not to laugh,' she said. 'I've had a word with her, and she's a nice, well-spoken little thing. I think she'll be just what we want.'

The three at the farm settled down into peaceful domesticity. To everyone's surprise, for Mona had only been singing her praises to save her own face, Silly Lizzie turned out, within limits, to be the paragon for which she was vaunted. She did everything she was told. The only drawback to her was that she did nothing she wasn't told, however obvious. Told to roast a leg of mutton for an hour and forty minutes, she roasted it for an hour and forty minutes, and very good it was. But left alone with the chops for supper, she roasted them for an hour and forty minutes also, with results that can be guessed. However, provided she got the supervision she needed, she was the perfect servant.

Jelkes was watching over Mona intently. She was entirely absorbed in regulating the menage. Before she broke out and took to art, she had had a thoroughly sound North Country upbringing, and now that she found herself responsible for the running of a household, all her old house-craft, so resented in the learning, returned to her. Jelkes knew that the household machine Mona was so laboriously getting into running order would fall to bits the moment her hand was removed. Lizzie and Bill would do anything for her, but without her they would slow up, come to a standstill. Monks Farm would be chaos when Mona left it.

Mr Pinker was getting towards the end of his activities for the moment. There were no internal decorations to do because everything was plain worked stone. When the muck was excavated from the cloister garth, they came, eighteen inches below the surface, upon the broken flag-stones of what had once been a paved courtyard. These, re-laid, made a fine crazy paving. Once the gutters were up Hugh had an inspiration, and led the rain-water from the roof to a lily-pool in the centre of the garth. Then they all packed into the car and went off to a near-by nursery, and if Mona had not been exceedingly firm, not to say a trifle caustic, Hugh would have had the entire stock sold to him, including all the old shrubs too big to move. Jelkes watched it all, and wondered where the pair of them were going to end. Hugh leant his weight on Mona, and Mona watched over his interests with the eye of a hawk. As Jelkes could see, Hugh and Mona were settling down to platonic domesticity. All the same, he had his doubts. He knew his Mona. She had no delusions, even if Hugh had.

And the sands were running out. Jelkes couldn't stop on indefinitely. As he truly said, 'I don't believe in spending too much energy on money-making, but a business is like a baby – you've got to attend to it sometimes, or you have trouble with it.'

But into their Eden the Serpent irrupted, for from a big Daimler descended Lady Paston; her eldest daughter, Lady Whitney; her younger daughter, the Hon. Mrs Fouldes, and an urbane, professional-looking gentleman who was not Dr Johnson. That fact alone filled Jelkes with profound uneasiness. For if it had merely been Hugh's health they were concerned about, the person in whom they would have trusted would have been the family physician who knew him. Two signatures, and only two, are necessary on the certificate that loses a man his freedom. If he had had his way, he would not have permitted the newcomer to set eyes on Hugh, for a man may only certify on what he sees, but Silly Lizzie showed the whole party in on top of them without demur.

Hugh looked distinctly annoyed, but was polite after the first surprise. Mona was introduced, and received with freezing coldness; Jelkes was introduced, and repaid the coldness with interest. The three women sat round like small boys at a pig-killing, and the doctor began to chat to Hugh, getting him on to the subject of Ambrosius almost without preamble. Jelkes wondered how he knew what to look for. Had Mrs Macintosh been indiscreet or unfaithful? Hugh, on his absorbing topic, opened up and forgot his constraint, and Jelkes marvelled at his unsuspiciousness.

Lady Paston then suggested a family conclave on business matters. Hugh sighed, but agreed.

Jelkes rose. He couldn't very well do anything else. He looked at the only other person present who wasn't a member of the family, and said: 'Perhaps Dr Hughes would care to join me in a stroll while family matters are being discussed?'

Dr Hughes blinked at this mode of address, for he had been introduced as plain Mr Hughes. He bowed politely, however.

'I am afraid I shall be needed,' he said, 'if you will excuse me.'

His manners were perfect, and Jelkes did not love him any better on that account. Sulkily he withdrew, and walked up and down outside the window so that he could hear if voices were raised in altercation; for he knew that if, having turned his mind on to Ambrosius, they baited Hugh up with a family row, they would probably get Ambrosius, which he guessed was what they wanted. Profoundly uneasy, he walked up and down, glancing in through the lighted window each time he passed.

Hugh was uneasy too; quite apart from the fact that his family always made him uneasy when they descended on him in bulk for the purposes of a family counsel; the peculiar sensitiveness that is the heritage of all negative natures told him that something out of the ordinary was afoot today. The ladies of the party, however, seemed quite indifferent to the tension in the atmosphere.

'Won't you sit down, Hugh?' said Lady Paston with that acid sweetness that had taken the place of authority since he had got too large to be smacked. 'We have been very worried about you.'

'You had no need to be,' muttered Hugh sulkily.

'We are very uneasy about these people you have got in with. We have had inquiries made about them, and they are not at all satisfactory. I suppose you know that the old man is an unfrocked priest?'

'No, he isn't,' said Hugh. 'He just didn't go on with his training.'

'We have heard otherwise.'

Hugh sat miserably silent, knowing the uselessness of argument, and quite unable to argue, even if it had been any use.

'I wonder whether you also know that the girl has got a very dubious reputation?'

Hugh sat up and looked her in the eye.

'I know nothing whatever about her history,' he said. 'I have always found her straight to deal with, and that is good enough for me.'

'What terms are you on with these people, Hugh? It seems to us a most extraordinary menage.'

'Jelkes is just a pal of mine,' he said. 'Miss Wilton is a kind of adopted daughter of his whom he looks after as she's got nobody else. She's a designer and house furnisher by trade and has been doing this job for me. It's only temporary,' he added desperately, feeling his heart sink within him at the words.

'I'm not so sure of that,' said Lady Paston. 'You may find it a lot easier to get her in than to get her out.'

Hugh mumbled a disclaimer, wishing to God that she were right.

'What does she get for whatever it is she is doing for you?' pursued Lady Paston.

'She gets a salary,' said Hugh.

'And the old man?'

'He gets nothing. He's here on holiday.'

'And what are you going to do with the girl when he goes home after his holiday? Is she going to stop on here with you?'

Hugh knew no more than she did, and continued to stare miserably into space.

'That is a matter on which I have no comment to make,' said Lady Paston. 'The day is long past when one even pretends to be shocked at such things. I have no doubt it is much better for you than sitting and brooding – isn't that so, Dr Hughes?'

'Oh, yes, yes, much better,' said Dr Hughes hastily. 'Never repress, always abreact your complexes.'

'What we are troubled about, however, and very troubled about indeed,' continued Lady Paston, 'is what will happen to you, Hugh, in the hands of these harpies. We have had so much of this sort of thing. You are so easily influenced. Anybody can get anything they like out of you.'

'There's plenty for everybody,' said Hugh sullenly.

'Not if you fritter it away. I have only a life interest, there is nothing I can leave your sisters. And there are Alice's two children, and Letitia's three, and Moira's baby.'

'Well, what about them? Won't they ever be able to earn a living? Have I got to support them permanently? Isn't anybody ever going to get a job?'

'You know perfectly well how difficult things have been for everybody. Surely you are prepared to make some provision for your sisters' children?'

'I should have thought their own fathers might have done something in that line.'

'There is no need to be offensive, Hugh. Now this is my suggestion, my dear boy, and as it is unlikely that I shall be with you very much longer, I hope you will do it to please me, and then we can all be happy together for the few short years that remain to me. I suggest that you make your affairs into a trust, Hugh, with Robert and Cosmo as the trustees; then capital cannot be frittered away, and there will be something for everybody. If I had known you were going to turn out as you have, I would never have persuaded your father to leave everything to you. If you can't make a mark in the world yourself, you might at least enable others to do so. What do you propose to leave your money to, Hugh, if not to the girls?'

'Hang it all, mother, why do they expect to get more out of it if there is a trust, with their husbands as trustees? Are the trustees proposing to misapply trust funds?'

'Hugh, you are not to speak like that, I won't have it. It is only to prevent the capital from being frittered away. You might just as well get things settled, Hugh, and then we can all be easy in our minds. What can you possibly leave your money to, if not to your sisters' children?'

'Has it never occurred to you that I might marry again?'

There was a dead silence. 'I thought as much,' said Lady Paston, at length. 'So she has got you to that point, has she?'

'Will she have you, Hugh?' came the voice of his youngest sister from his left.

'Judging on type, I should say she wouldn't,' came the voice of his eldest sister from his right. 'She looks to me a passionate, full-blooded type. Personally I shouldn't think she would have you if you were the last man left alive.'

Hugh was too bitterly appreciative of the truths contained in these remarks to realize the *volte-face* they indicated.

His mother's voice interrupted his thoughts as he sat staring out of the window into the fast deepening twilight, oblivious of his companions, who were watching him like so many cats at a mouse-hole.

'We would be only too happy for you to marry, dear,' she said, 'provided the girl was suitable; but you are very foolish to involve yourself with this Wilton woman, who believe me, is more than unsuitable. We have had inquiries made about her, and quite apart from being very middle-class indeed, she has led a thoroughly loose life, living with various men.'

'I don't suppose she'd marry me even for my money,' said Hugh bitterly, and the company pricked up its ears as one man.

'Have you asked her?' asked Lady Paston tartly.

'No,' said Hugh.

'Are you going to?'

'I don't know. I think not.'

Then all of a sudden something seemed to snap like a harp-string inside Hugh's head; for a moment the room swam round him; then it steadied again and he gathered his wits together; but they were not the wits of Hugh, but of Ambrosius.

The two minds overlapped, like two exposures on the same film, and the resulting man was neither one thing nor the other. There came upon him a horrible nightmare feeling of confusion and bewilderment. He did not know where he was – and yet the place was familiar. He did not know who these people were, and yet their faces were not strange. He knew, however, with both sides of his mind, that he was in a very tight corner, but what his peril was he could not be sure.

He knew that a net was closing round him, that suspicion was hardening into certainty; that the power of Rome had been invoked by certain of the senior monks, and that at any moment one who could not be denied might arrive. But these people did not look like the delegation from Rome; then who were they? He was utterly perplexed, dreading a misstep that might precipitate the very danger he was striving desperately to ward off. But whatever else was unreal, he knew that the danger was real, and he felt the cold hand of fear on throat and heart.

But whereas in this crisis Hugh would have been as helpless as a bird before a snake, something that was not Hugh was also present, and as they watched him they saw his face change, and there was looking at them a man who, whoever he might be, was certainly not Hugh. Dr Hughes, too experienced to precipitate a crisis, kept quiet and took mental notes. He was familiar with the classical cases of dual personality, and had seen some minor ones in his own experience, but he had never come across anything like this before. The personality that was now present was putting the fear of God into him in a way that no pathology ought to do.

Then there came to the man standing there in the midst of them the knowledge that he was broken – that this was the end. Those who sat round him, whoever they might be, were the representatives of a power he could not resist; the inner protection that had been his ever since he had first contacted the great Goat-Foot God was withdrawn, and he waited for death unarmed.

Then he knew with an inner certainty that there was that in the soul which could rise above the bondage of the age and go free. Outwardly he had failed, but on the inner planes he had made the conditions that would assure success at the next attempt. He would go now, and he would come again. He would offer no resistance against his accusers; he would not take refuge in flight. The inner resistance withdrawn, they could take his life and be done with it. But in his heart were the promises that had been made to him in the strange visions and writings that had been his. When he came again, conditions would be right; the god would manifest as promised: the dreams would come true.

Then there arose in him an overmastering desire to go once again to his own place, his priory. He walked boldly out of the door, and none stayed him.

He turned and went towards the chapel. He would stand in the centre of the great Sign that showed forth the created universe. He would stand at the point of the concourse of forces, and there he would surrender his soul to the powers that created it.

Someone spoke to him as he crossed the dew-soaked grass to the chapel door; he did not know who it was, but the feel of the man was friendly, so it must be one of his own monks, not the strangers from Rome with their Italian subtlety and cruelty. He gave the curt blessing of peace expected of an ecclesiastic of his grade, and passed on and entered the darkness of the chapel.

As he took the great doors in his hands to close them, he stood still and looked back. The sun had set, but the afterglow lingered in the sky over the dark trees, at its verge one silver star. He stood long and looked at it. He would not see it again, he knew that. He had a strange feeling as if it had all happened before – as if he knew exactly what was coming. They would seek him here; they would take him down underground; and before dawn death would find him.

He went up through the darkness to the high altar and took his stand as he had planned. Around him were the symbols of the heavenly houses; behind him the great Regents of the Elements, winged like archangels, stood in their buttressing bays. He stood for a while, and then knelt down and laid his hands on the cubical altar of stone. Those who would come for him should find him here.

Back in the room he had left, a rather heated conference was in progress. 'Do you think,' said Lady Paston, 'that you can certify on what you have seen?'

Dr Hughes rubbed his chin. 'It's a little difficult. I should have liked to have had something more definite. One has to be so very careful.'

'Well, I should have thought we had seen enough today for anybody to certify on. I never saw anything that looked madder in my life.'

'Yes, but he hasn't *done* anything, dear lady.'

'It isn't what he does. He has never done anything in his life – and never will—' said Lady Paston bitterly. 'It is what other people do when they get him into their hands. Dr Johnson is prepared to certify him, if you are, and he knows him very well.'

'Mm. Ah. One has to be very careful.'

'Well, if you don't certify him, there won't be a penny left for anybody. Quite subnormal mentally, Dr Johnson tells me.'

'Mm. Ah. Yes.'

'Well, what do you suggest?' Lady Paston was beginning to get a little tart. Dr Hughes had been brought for a special purpose, and knew it, but he did not seem disposed to get on with the job.

'Of course if I had Mr Paston under my care for a time—'

'That's no use,' snapped Lady Paston. 'That won't enable us to take his affairs in hand and look after them.'

'I think we had better have another opinion,' said Lady Whitney icily.

'Since the matter is somewhat urgent,' said Dr Hughes hastily, seeing his very considerable consultant's fee in sudden danger, 'it might, on the whole, be in his best interests to certify him. There do not seem to be any difficulties in the way. I will have a word with Dr Johnson, and see what he thinks. He has known him longer than I have. If he thinks it advisable, I will not say no.'

So all arrangements were made once more for walling Hugh up alive, and history was about to repeat itself, when in walked Jelkes and stood in the centre of the circle with his hands on his hips, glaring at them.

'What the hell do you think you're playing at?' he demanded of Dr Hughes, who jumped as if he had had a pin stuck in him.

'My dear sir, my dear sir, I don't know what you are talking about, but your tone is most offensive. I must really take exception to it.'

'Have you had your ear to the keyhole?' snapped Hugh's youngest sister.

'No, not the keyhole; but the window is open and you've all got voices like peacocks.'

Dr Hughes turned to his female companions. 'I think, dear ladies, we might as well be going. There is nothing more we can do for the moment.'

Jelkes went hastily to the chapel as the dying sounds of the car assured him that they had really gone. He saw, kneeling in front of the altar that was not a Christian altar, the figure of a man, and that man, whoever he might be, was calling upon strange gods.

Jelkes groaned, withdrew quietly, and returned to the house.

He called to Mona, who had retreated to her bedroom under the irruption of Hugh's womenfolk, and told her what had happened. Ambrosius had arrived in front of witnesses – hostile witnesses. It was at this moment, as they were debating the gloomy prospect, that the sounds of a car on the drive were heard once more.

'My God!' said Jelkes. 'What is it now?'

He went to the door, and there confronted a short, dapper, elderly man, who got out of a coupé as neat and small as himself.

'Good evening,' he said. 'Is Mr Paston at home?'

'No, he isn't,' said Jelkes curtly, eyeing him with unconcealed hostility, at which the newcomer looked rather taken aback.

'That's a pity,' he said. 'I thought I could have saved him a trip into town. I have just been with Miss Pumfrey, getting her signature, and I thought perhaps I could get his, and hand over the deeds and be done with it. Perhaps you would be good enough to ask him to call at my office at his convenience. My name is Watney.'

Jelkes looked at him for a moment. 'Is it?' he said. 'Come inside,' and held the door open.

Mr Watney entered, and passed into the living-room, where he saw Mona, obviously agitated, standing before the fire. He sensed the tenseness of the atmosphere, and noted the absence of Hugh.

'Sit down,' said Jelkes curtly. 'We're in the devil of a mess.'

Mr Watney looked at him inquiringly, but with true legal caution uttered no comment.

'This is the position, sir,' said Jelkes. 'My friend Hugh Paston, has recently been through a good deal of trouble – lost his wife in rather tragic circumstances.'

Watney nodded. He evidently knew.

'The result has been to upset him a good deal, and to bring on – er – split personality. I dare say you have heard of such things?'

'Yes, I have heard of them,' said the man of law, dry and non-committal.

'There are times—' Jelkes struggled on, 'when he shifts from his normal self into a – er – secondary personality.'

'And the time at the museum was one of them,' said Watney, looking at Mona. 'I knew that wasn't an ordinary faint.'

'The point is this,' said Jelkes. 'In my opinion, and I know something of abnormal psychology, Hugh will soon right himself. But the trouble is, his family seem to want to get him certified.'

'Why should they wish to do that, if it is not necessary?'

'Because if he were certified, they would have the control of a very large estate, and his sisters' children, would come in for it. Whereas, if he remains at large and – er – should marry again, he might have children, and then his children would inherit.'

'Is he likely to marry again?'

Jelkes hesitated.

'Not that I know of,' said Mona.

Something, he could not say what, made Mr Watney look behind him, the others followed his glance, and there, in the doorway, stood Hugh, and, Jelkes thanked his stars, it was Hugh, and not Ambrosius.

'I am afraid I have been an involuntary eavesdropper for the bulk of your conversation,' said Hugh, coming slowly into the room. He never looked at Mona.

'Then,' said Jelkes, 'you know the lie of the land?'

Hugh turned to the solicitor. 'Well, Mr Watney, it looks as if I were in for a life sentence if I don't watch my step. What about it? You are a man of law, can you suggest anything?'

'I can only suggest that you consult your lawyer and your family physician, Mr Paston.'

'That would be just walking into the lion's den. It is our family physician who is in on this thing. As for my lawyers, well, I don't know. I shouldn't be surprised if I were worth more to them locked up than loose.'

'Is there no person, no friend of the family, of your late father for instance, upon whose disinterestedness you can rely?'

Hugh waved his hand towards the old bookseller.

'Jelkes, here,' he said. 'I don't know of another soul. Unless, maybe—?' he looked at Mona and hesitated.

'I would do what I could,' said Mona quietly.

'I am glad to have that assurance,' said Hugh, 'and I shan't—' he hesitated, seeking the word that would express what he meant, 'I shan't overstep my welcome.'

There was high tension in the atmosphere, and everybody felt acutely embarrassed.

Jelkes broke it. 'Do you know what I should **do**, if I were you, Hugh? I should take your affairs out of the hands of your solicitors, if you don't feel you can trust 'em, and get Mr Watney to look after them for you.'

'That's just what was in my mind,' said Hugh. 'That is, if Mr Watney is willing?'

'Er – well, of course I should be very pleased. Who wouldn't be? But – er – family lawyers, Mr Paston? Things may be complicated. Did your father tie things up with them in any way?'

'Not with these lawyers. I shifted to them to please my wife. She couldn't abide the others. Had no end of a row with them. We disentangled all the legal knots then. I haven't been with these folk much over three years.'

'Then in that case, I shall be very pleased to take charge of your affairs, though I should have felt some diffidence in taking them out of the hands of family lawyers.'

'And I'd like you to have them,' said Hugh, suddenly smiling at him. The little old bachelor beamed back. Hugh had pulled off his stunt once more. Mr Watney had followed Mrs Pascoe into the cohort of those who looked after Hugh far better than he could look after himself.

'Now, Mr Paston,' said the little lawyer, suddenly losing his diffidence and becoming authoritative. 'I should advise you to give me the necessary authority to take over all your papers from your present firm, and I will send a clerk up first thing tomorrow morning, before they know what is afoot, and collect 'em. Possession is nine points of the law. Secondly, if you feel sufficient confidence in us, I suggest that you give me your Power of Attorney, to come into effect in the event of your incapacity. They'll contest that, of course, if we ever have to use it, which I hope we won't. But again, possession is nine points of the law, and they will have to dislodge us from an entrenched position. A High Court job, Mr Paston. Plenty of publicity. The right counsel could make 'em wish they were dead.'

He beamed at them all through his horn-rimmed glasses, in his element.

'What is the point in giving you Power of Attorney?' said Mona curtly.

'It is this, Miss Wilton. Supposing they did certify Mr Paston, they would not obtain control of his affairs without a tremendous struggle. I'd fight them tooth and nail through every court in the country. They'll know that, without being told. I think you will find that as soon as they know there is a Power of Attorney in existence, they will drop the idea of certification, especially if Mr Paston places himself in the hands of a doctor.'

'I think that's O.K.,' said Hugh. 'Who'll we get for the disinterested doctor? Mrs Macintosh's husband's cousin?'

'No,' said Mona decisively. 'He's all right for a cold on the chest, no one better, but he'd be no good for this job. He'd be like Mrs Macintosh, incredulous and scared at the same time.'

Mr Watney pricked up his ears. He had sensed all along that there was much more in the whole transaction than met the eye.

'Now that I am definitely acting for you, Mr Paston,' he said, 'I suggest you run up to town first thing tomorrow morning and see someone really first-class, whose opinion cannot be gainsaid.'

'No,' said Jelkes. 'We'll have the local saw-bones in tonight. I'm taking no chances.'

'I know the man we want,' continued Mr Watney. 'A young chap who's just set up in the district. He'll be very pleased to have a patient from me and will do as I tell him. You leave it to me. I'll send him along on my way back.'

Having speeded the parting guest, Jelkes returned to the living-room to find that Mona had disappeared. She had evidently got no mind for a *tête à tête* with Hugh in his present state. Jelkes sat down and had a good look at him, and what he saw, he did not like. He seemed suddenly to have aged in a very curious manner. He had the look, as if of a man whose work is over and who is waiting for death.

'Well, Hugh, what are you going to do? Are you going to push on with the furnishing of this place under the circumstances?'

Hugh roused himself with an effort.

'I am sure I don't know. Hadn't thought about it,' he replied. 'Miss Wilton can get whatever's needful.'

They sat for a while in silence, and then a car was heard once more on the drive.

'That'll be Watney's saw-bones,' said Jelkes.

He proved to be a young fellow, masking nervousness under over-assurance. He stood looking at his patient in silence for a moment. 'Mr Watney asked me to come and see you. I am Dr Atkins.'

'Very good of you, I'm sure,' said Hugh, and conversation languished, Dr Atkins trying desperately to remember what had been taught him in his scanty instruction in the law relating to certification.

'Er, can you tell me what day of the week it is?' he said at length.

'It's been Wednesday all day long, so far as I know,' said Hugh, and silence fell again.

Dr Atkins felt himself beginning to perspire. This was his first important case in his first start in practice, and he was hashing it horribly. He felt he knew even less about psychiatry than he did about midwifery.

'May I examine you?' he said at length, hoping to warm up on the accustomed routine.

'Certainly,' said Hugh. 'Anything you like.'

Dr Atkins got out his stethoscope.

'Would you be good enough to undress?'

'Undress?' exclaimed Hugh, suddenly waking up. 'Good Lord, man, I'm all right from the neck downwards. This is where my trouble is,' and he tapped his head. 'You don't want to stethoscope that, do you? Come and sit down and have a cigarette.'

'Thanks,' said Dr Atkins, feeling he was showing tact.

'I don't know what we've got in the way of refreshments,' said Hugh, 'I am afraid there's nothing but bottled beer,' and produced some forthwith from the sideboard. Dr Atkins, what with gratitude for the beer and relief at the turn the interview had taken, forgot to be professional and became the decent, inexperienced lad Nature meant him to be.

It was Hugh who took charge of the interview.

'I suppose Mr Watney told you all there is to tell?' he said.

'He told me all he knew,' said Dr Atkins, grinning. 'But I dare say there's plenty more if you care to tell it.'

'I suppose Watney told you they want to certify me? I dare say they're right, but I don't want to be certified. I'd be glad if you could fix it so that I'm not. I'll do anything you want me to.'

Dr Atkins, warmed by the beer, began to feel as if he were under Divine guidance, so successful did he appear to be in the management of mental cases.

'Don't you worry about that,' he said. 'I'll see you're not certified.'

'Have some more beer?' said Hugh.

'Thanks, I will,' said Dr Atkins.

Hugh opened another bottle. 'Know anything about psychoanalysis?'

'No, not much.'

'Well, I do,' said Hugh. 'And I'll wring your neck if you try it on me.'

'Right-o,' said Dr Atkins.

And so they parted. Hugh greatly relieved. He liked Dr Atkins personally, and had had his fears laid to rest. Dr Atkins, for his part, drove straight home and looked up the case in his books before he put the car away. He knew he had succeeded, but he did not know how, or why.

Jelkes mounted guard over the household all the following day, and the next, but no sign came from the hostile camp. As Mr Watney had surmised, the Power of Attorney stymied them neatly, and they dropped the idea of certification, for the moment, at any rate, and unless Hugh did something really outrageous, he was safe enough.

But even if that sword no longer hung over their heads, there was still a pretty serious problem on their hands, for it could not be denied that there was something very much wrong with Hugh. He had lapsed into a peculiar, brooding, spiritless apathy, as if his mind were away in another world and that world not a pleasant one. Jelkes, who had read widely in psychology and had seen a good many cracked-up minds among the Jesuits – a nervous breakdown, politely called surrender to God, being part of their curriculum – didn't like the look of Hugh at all. He had a shrewd suspicion, judging him on type, that he would swing between apathy and excitability. Jelkes was deadly uneasy at the idea of leaving Mona alone with Hugh, but for the life of him did not see how he could let his business take care of itself any longer if he expected to have any business left to go back to.

CHAPTER SEVEN

By the end of the week Hugh seemed considerably more normal. The telephone was in, so in case of emergency Mona could get either Mr Watney, the doctor, or the police according to which seemed to be indicated. Jelkes decided to risk it, and leave Monks Farm to its own devices for a few days and see what was happening to his means of livelihood. Hugh ran him down into the valley in the car, and he caught the evening bus for London.

Having pushed Jelkes into his bus Hugh put the big car about and drove up into the hills. He dreaded the first meeting with Mona alone. There was a lot to be thought out. He needed to be clear on his own line of action, and very sure of his ability to carry it out. It was going to take a good deal of self-control, he thought, to go just so far and no further, and not slip into anything that would earn him a snub from Mona, which might cause him, in his strung-up state, to lose his temper and have a row with her that would lead to permanent estrangement.

The thing he feared was the loss of his own self-control. He had always known that he had no stomach for a fight, that he was as weak as ditch-water in every relationship of life, but now he found himself getting his head down and going at things like a bull at a gate. He knew the thing his whole being ached for – life, more life, fullness of life – the blessing of Pan!

All around him, where he had pulled up his car on the high common, the gorse was in flower, and its sweet almondy odour filled the air. There was a mellowness as of summer in the slow-moving wind of the warm spring dusk. April was ending; May would soon be here; and with the last day of April came the Eve of Beltane.

According to tradition Beltane was the Night of the Witches, and if anything were going to happen, it might be expected to happen then. He wondered what form Pan would take if he appeared? Would he come crudely, as a materializing stench of goat? Or would he come more subtly in the soul?

He, for his part, did not know quite what to expect, and so could not decide whether he should be disappointed that more that was spectacular had not happened, or satisfied that so much had already come about. Looking back over the weeks that had passed since he had started to break out of the luminous opacity that was his opal, he could not deny that things had happened – Ambrosius, for instance – and Mona had come into his life, with results that looked as if they were going to prove harrowing.

Was all this the fruit of his invocation of Pan? He began to suspect that it was. For after all, what was an invocation of Pan, in the first instance, save a resolution to break out of the opal? He had given permission to his own subconscious to come up to the light. Then he had gone on to invoke the primordial forces of life to declare themselves. Not only had he let loose the Pan within, but he had called upon the Great God Pan without. Plenty of people let loose the Pan within – the most appropriate rite for that was alcoholic – but the Great God Pan – that was another matter. But was the Great God evil? 'No!' said Hugh aloud. 'He isn't. I repudiate that.'

And with that he started the engine, and put the car about once more, and returned to Monks Farm and Mona.

As he came over a rise in the ground that hid the farm from the road and saw the firelight shining out of its uncurtained windows, he felt an exquisite pleasure, and at the same time a tantalized sense of frustration. The car slid down the gentle slope and he eased it through the wide doors of the barn as silently as a ghost. The newly-rolled gravel hardly crunched, and Hugh returned to his home unobserved.

He cut across the courtyard from the barn, intending to enter by the back door. As he passed the kitchen window he glanced in, and saw there Bill, very much taking his ease by the fire, with Silly Lizzie worshipping him as if he were the Vision Beautiful. Hugh hesitated. To break in on an idyll like that was like smashing a pane of glass. He turned away, re-crossing the courtyard, and entered the chapel.

It was as black as pitch at first, but the lingering after-glow gleamed faintly through the west window, and his eyes gradually became accustomed to the dim light. The great angels in the buttressing bays were hidden in the gloom, but the dark mass of the Tree on the high wall at the eastern end showed up against its lighter background. Hugh stood staring at it, trying to picture it as he knew it to be, with its ten gaudy fruit arranged in their three symmetrical triangles with the odd one at the bottom. He had heard Jelkes dis-course of the symbolism of that Tree, representing heaven and earth and the intermediate worlds between, according to the ancient rabbis. He moved slowly up the broad space of the nave, mounted the three shallow steps, and felt under his feet the smooth tessellated pavement of the sanctuary. Around him, though hidden by the darkness, was the rude circle of the Zodiac as designed by the primitive mosaic-workers of Ambrosius' day. His feet were treading the actual flooring that had been trodden by the sandalled feet of the dead monk. He wondered how often Ambrosius had come in thus, alone in the darkness, seeking guidance and strength as the net closed round him, and he thought how narrow his own escape had been from the spiritual equivalent of being walled up alive. He tried to reconstruct in his imagination the cubical altar of the Templars, which, according to their enemies, was the obscene throne of the goat-god, but accord-ing to themselves merely symbolized the universe.

He could imagine Ambrosius by sheer will-power domi-nating any one who came his way. And as he thought, imagining the mind of Ambrosius, it seemed to him as if something in his own mind opened like a door, and the two minds coincided, and once again he *was* Ambrosius. But this time he knew it. There was no closing-down of the one consciousness as the other opened, they were intercommuni-cating for a brief second.

But the door closed again as swiftly as it had opened. Hugh breathless and sweating, staggered slightly as he recovered his balance. But now he understood a good many things he had not understood before. He realized that he did not 'get' Ambrosius by concentrating on a mental picture of him, as he had tried to do in the stuffy little parlour at the Green Man, but by meditating on what Ambrosius must have felt or thought or done. The thing in Hugh stirred in its sleep and chuckled. A key had been found, if he had the nerve to use it. Ambrosius could be invoked at will by simply identifying with him. He must not just merely *look* at Ambrosius – he must *be* Ambrosius.

Exactly what the consequences would be, he did not know, but suspected that they might be drastic. He might even get himself certified in good earnest if he went on like this. But he did not care. He didn't care a damn for the consequences. The renegade ecclesiastic had already begun to leave his mark behind him.

Hugh turned and left the chapel and made his way round to the south front of the priory, passing silently over the dew-soaked grass. Glancing in at the window as he passed, he saw Mona sitting over the fire, an unlit lamp beside her, her elbows on her knees and her chin in her hands, staring into the flames, deep in thought. And anxious thought, too, to judge by the set of her mouth and the lines on her forehead. The door stood open to the mild spring night and he entered unheard. It was not till he spoke to her that she realized his presence, and then she leapt to her feet so startled that she sent her chair over behind her.

'I'm sorry,' he said. 'I didn't mean to scare you like that.'

'It's very stupid of me,' said Mona. 'I don't know why I jumped like that. I can't imagine.'

But he knew perfectly well, and so did she. It was the hawk face in the black cowl she dreaded to see.

'This is rather awkward,' said Hugh, dropping into his accustomed chair. 'Sit down, Mona, we've got to face up to this, otherwise we shall never be able to exist together in the same house. You're not scared of me, are you? No one on

God's earth could be scared of me. Is it Ambrosius you're scared of?'

'Yes, perhaps I am; but all the same he has got to come through.'

Mona sat silent for quite a while, staring at the fire, and Hugh sat watching her. He could imagine Ambrosius watching like that, from the window in the Abbey gate-house that overlooked the market-place – watching the women that were forbidden to him as a Churchman.

Mona seemed to have forgotten Hugh's presence, and he sat watching her in the dying firelight, wondering whether he dared think of Ambrosius, or whether, if he did, he would wreck the whole show. For a moment it seemed to him that he could almost see with his physical eyes the arched stone mullions of the gate-house window through which he looked.

At length she spoke once more. 'Hugh, has it ever occurred to you to wonder exactly what Ambrosius is?'

'Well, I took it for granted that I'm more or less medium-istic, without ever having realized it, and that a dead monk would speak through me, given half a chance.'

'That's one possibility,' said Mona. 'Ever heard Uncle Jelkes speak of reincarnation?'

'Yes, I've heard him talk, but I'm not sure I took in very much of it. He's too metaphysical for me. But anyway, what about it? Supposing I was Ambrosius in a past life, what do I do about it in this one?'

'That was just what I was puzzling over,' she said. 'So far as I can see, the only thing for you to do is to face up to Ambrosius, and then absorb him. Only I don't quite know how it is to be done.'

'I do, though,' said Hugh. 'I have only got to think of myself as him, and feel him strongly, and I *am* him. I've done it several times for brief moments.'

'If you do that,' said Mona, 'Ambrosius will absorb you instead of your absorbing him.'

'I shouldn't object to that,' said Hugh, 'he's a sight better specimen than I am. I believe you'd like Ambrosius a lot better than you like me, Mona. Oddly enough, you know, it's through you I always get into touch with Ambrosius. He missed a lot in life, and so have I; and it's when I get comparing what I have missed with what Ambrosius missed that I get in touch with him.'

Mona did not offer any comment.

Hugh spoke again:

'Do you know what I shall do, Mona, if things turn out all right? I shall ask you if you'll marry me. Now don't you start getting worried. There's no need for you to go to the trouble of refusing me, for I'm not asking you now. But if things straighten out for me, I shall come and ask you.'

They both did more thinking than sleeping that night. Mona had said more than she had meant to, and was very worried in consequence. With the suggestion of reincarnation Hugh had been started off on a line of ideas that would bear fruit in the near future. Any wavering or uncertainty in handling him, and there would be a crash.

Hugh's suggestion of marriage she did not take seriously. She was not in the least attracted by him, though she liked him and was exceedingly sorry for him. She was old enough, and disillusioned enough, to consider the possibility of marrying for the sake of a home, but they came from such totally different worlds. None of his friends would accept her, and she would loathe his way of life. She could not play bridge: she had not a notion how to give a dinner-party, or even how to attend one; and as for a week-end at a country house, it would be the death of her. She could neither dress nor walk nor talk as did the women of his world, and her dignity was a thing that Mona valued highly.

She cast her mind back to the scene of Greece about which Hugh had told her, and of the sun-drenched hill-side above the sea where he had followed a woman clad in a fawn-skin who had had her carriage and walk. Mona, who was well read in modern psychology, knew at once what Hugh's subconscious had said in that dream. But she also knew that such a scene as this had been a favourite phantasy of hers all through her childhood and girlhood. As a child she had daydreamed of racing over sun-warmed rocks beside a boy-comrade, clad in the short Spartan tunic she had seen in her book of Greek legends. As she grew older, the phantasy had grown more romantic, and it was the pursuit of the lover, not the hand in hand running of comrades that she phantasied. Later, when Jelkes introduced her to the knowledge of the ancient Mysteries and what was taught at Eleusis, the phantasy took on yet another content, and she visualized herself as the maenad adoring Dionysus, giver of ecstasy, and following the beautiful god over the mountains in the frenzied running dance.

It was odd that Hugh should have had the same phantasy in his dream but she must not take the shared phantasy as indicative of twin soulery. That was merely asking for trouble. It was quite a tricky enough business even when handled impersonally, and utterly impossible if she let her feelings in any way become involved.

Remembering Hugh's reactions in his dream, and the face of Ambrosius when he appeared in the upper room of the museum, Mona considered the possibility of some fairly drastic experiences before they had got Hugh safely onto his feet. Remembering Freud's dictum that cure proceeds via transference, she faced the possibility of having to become Hugh's mistress for a time, and concluded that it wouldn't kill her if she had to. Mona cared nothing for conventions and had her own ideas on the subject of morals. She was not a sensual woman, but she would give herself for love freely, and under whatever conditions she saw fit; and oddly enough, she would also give herself out of pity if the need were great enough.

Hugh, for his part, stood in front of his low-pitched window with his hands in his pockets staring out into the moonlight hour after hour, totally unconscious of the lapse of time. He saw the Greek hill-side and knew that the woman he had been pursuing was beyond all question Mona, and wondered whether in a still earlier incarnation he had enacted just such a scene. He saw Ambrosius walking around the priory as it was a-building, just as he himself had walked around it while it was being restored. He thought of the discovery he had made in the chapel of the trick of looking out of Ambrosius' hood in order to become Ambrosius.

This checked the flight of his imagination and gave him a

cold feeling all down his spine. If it came off, what the devil would happen? He did not care what happened to himself. The thing that worried him was what he might do to Mona Wilton. He had no confidence in Ambrosius' morals. He judged that that repressed celibate would break out pretty badly once he started, and whether he were the result of Greek magic in the past or a marriage gone wrong in the present, the consequences would be the same.

In the morning Mona met a dispirited Hugh at breakfast, and could have shaken him for the way in which his moods veered with the wind. So far as could be judged from his demeanour, yesterday's conversation might never have taken place. After breakfast he disappeared and she saw him no more.

Her household duties concluded, she took a note-book and measuring-rod and set out to plan the garden she intended to make inside the courtyard of the old farmhouse. There should also, she thought, be a wide double herbaceous border leading from the west door out across the pasture to the fir-wood, bordering the faint track that led thither and that was a favourite sunset stroll. There could be no question of stately hollyhocks and regal delphiniums in the shallow, stony soil upon the chalk, but grey, aromatic things such as sea-lavender and old man's beard; goat's rue and thrift; flowering sage, scarlet and blue, and southernwood and rosemary.

She went just inside the door of the chapel to make her notes and calculate her measurements. She was busily engaged in adding and subtracting when there stole over her a feeling that she was not alone. She glanced uneasily over her shoulder, cross with herself for being so nervous, and saw Hugh standing bolt upright and motionless in the centre of the crude Zodiac on the tessellated pavement of the sanctuary. That motionless, absorbed figure produced a very queer feeling as one watched it. She wondered whether it were Ambrosius or Hugh, or a blend of the two, and for some reason she could not define, inclined to the latter idea.

He stood in the centre of the circle of the Zodiac, his feet in a smaller circle which contained the signs of the four elements of earth, air, fire and water. In the compartments formed by the radii of the signs were small holes into which Mona knew the signs representing the seven planets could be fitted according to the manner in which they stood in their heavenly houses as the wheel of the skies revolved. Hugh was standing in the exact centre of the symbolic representation of the universe, and Mona thought that she had never believed it possible that any living being could be so absolutely alone.

All her irritation with Hugh vanished. He was the watery type, under the presidency of the Moon and Aquarius; it was his nature to be attentive to the wavering images reflected by moonlight on water. She herself was of the earth, being a Virgo, and Virgo is not Ever-virgin, but also Many-breasted.

She felt a profound pity for that lonely soul up there in the shadows of the east, unlighted by any window in the sanctuary, for Ambrosius, for some reason best known to himself, had left the eastern end of his church in darkness. She sat waiting, watching, and wondering. It seemed as if Hugh would stand there indefinitely. Finally she could bear the tension no longer, and moving silently she passed up the aisle and took her stand behind and a little to one side of him.

After a few moments he, like herself, became aware that he was not alone, looked over his shoulder, and saw her. He looked at her for a moment, and his face took on a very strange expression; melancholy, fatalistic, and yet with a touch of fire and fanaticism slumbering behind his eyes. She had a queer feeling that more than one pair of eyes were looking out from under Hugh's rather heavy lids.

They looked at each other without speaking. Speech was impossible. That was a silence that could not be broken. Then Hugh held out his hand and she put hers in it. Her unhesitating response sent a thrill through Hugh, and his face twitched in a manner that Mona knew was a sure indication that he was emotionally moved. Then he turned towards the East again, and drew her to stand beside him within the circle of the Elements, and they stood facing the altar that was not there, and which, if it had been theres would have been the throne of the goat-god, hand in hand, as if being married.

Mona's heart was beating hard in her throat. There was no knowing what was going to happen next. Ambrosius was capable of anything. Then gradually the panic fear passed away and its place was taken by a profound peace. Then the peace gave place to a curious tense thrilling, like a great organ-note sounding in the soul. Then that too gradually died away, and she knew that they were back to normal.

'Shall we go now?' she said, touching him lightly on the sleeve. He nodded, and fell into step beside her as they went down the aisle together. She felt a hand laid on her shoulder, looked up, and in the light of the doorway saw Hugh looking very lined and grey and worn and much more round-shouldered than usual.

'These things are tearing me to pieces, Mona,' he said in a low voice. 'God knows what will be the upshot of it.'

They sat down on a low bench in the angle of the wall, the heat of the spring sun warming them after the chill of the chapel; Hugh stretched out his long legs and put his hands behind his head and leant back and shut his eyes. Mona gazed at him anxiously. He looked absolutely done.

The obvious, common-sense remedy was for Hugh to refrain from playing about with Ambrosius any more. But Mona had a profound conviction that Hugh had got to work through Ambrosius and come out the other side if things were ever to be right with him, and that if he turned back now it would be to re-enter into the death-in-life that was closing about him when he had first come to the Marylebone bookshop.

At that moment they heard a footstep on the gravel, and Mr Watney appeared. Mona was never so pleased to see anyone in her life.

Hugh pulled himself together and did the polite. Produced cigarettes and went in search of whisky, leaving Mona and the solicitor together.

'Well?' said Mr Watney as soon as they were alone. 'And how is our friend?'

'I am rather bothered about him,' said Mona, 'and I don't feel that doctors would be the slightest use. You see, he's had a pretty bad shock. His wife was killed in a motor-smash, and it all came out about how she was carrying on with another man at the time. He had never suspected it and had absolutely believed in her.'

'How long ago was this?'

'It must be getting on for two months now.'

'Then I do not think that was the cause of the trouble, for he was not fond of her.'

'How do you know?'

'Because he is obviously very much in love with you.'

Mona was too worried to make the indignant repudiation. 'What makes you think that?' she asked soberly.

He looked at her sharply over his spectacles.

'Hadn't you seen that for yourself?'

'I had seen it, but I hadn't taken it seriously, knowing his type of man.'

'Then you have made a mistake. He is taking it very seriously. I was watching him when you said that there was no marriage in the offing the other afternoon. It was a knock-out blow for him. Whatever other troubles he may have, that is what is causing the flare-up now.'

'Oh dear, this is very awkward,' said Mona. 'I knew he wanted to flirt with me, but I had no idea it was as serious as all that. What's to be done about it?'

'Don't you care about him?'

'Not in that way. It wouldn't work.'

'Why not?'

'We belong to different worlds. We've got nothing in common. I'd never settle with him, and he'd never settle with me.'

'Well, I suppose you know your own business best, but I'm sorry. He's a nice fellow, and it would have been the salvation of him.'

At that moment Hugh returned with the drinks, shared the whisky with Mr Watney, and gave Mona a cocktail, which she was very glad to have.

They chatted in a desultory manner. Hugh invited Mr

Watney to lunch, which invitation was accepted, and Mona fled to see if there were enough food. It would never have entered Hugh's head to raise that point before issuing an invitation.

The moment she had turned the corner, Hugh's manner changed.

'I want to make a new will,' he said abruptly.

'Do you?' said the solicitor, wondering what was afoot now. 'If you can give me pencil and paper I'll jot down the headings and let you have a draft.'

An eighth of Hugh's personal estate was to go to his mother and to each of his three sisters. The remaining half was to be divided equally between Mona and Jelkes. Mona was to have Monks Farm. Mr Watney gasped. The papers had arrived from his predecessors, and he knew the size of that estate.

An hour later Mona called them to lunch. Everyone did their best, but it was not a cheery meal. After Mr Watney had gone Hugh sat over the fire in the little sitting-room smoking a big cigar that had been given him.

Mona wanted to talk to him, but found it difficult to make a start. Hugh paid no attention to her. The sun outside was shining gloriously, but he had got all the windows tight shut and was throwing logs on the fire.

'Why don't you come outside?' said Mona. 'It's a shame to leave this sunshine running to waste.'

'Too much trouble to move,' said Hugh, kicking a protruding log impatiently.

Mona, who had scant patience with spoilt children, cleared out and left him, hoping that, what with the large lunch and the many whiskies and the hot room, he would sleep himself sensible by tea-time.

When she returned from her walk as the early spring dusk closed in, Hugh said: 'I can't expect you to dry-nurse me indefinitely.'

Common sense bade her return an airy answer, but something that was not sensible welled up from deep in her, and she replied: 'We'll see this through together, Hugh.'

He made no acknowledgment.

'Tell me, what were you doing in the chapel this morning?' said Mona.

'Trying to work things out.'

'Did you get Ambrosius?'

'No, didn't try for him. To tell you the honest truth, Mona, I'm a bit scared of Ambrosius. You see, I feel that when he comes, he'll come with the hell of a rush, and I'm not sure that he's to be trusted.'

'I've got a notion I could handle Ambrosius,' said Mona. 'I'll tell you a curious thing, Hugh, do you know that this business goes back long before Ambrosius?'

'What do you mean?'

'Do you remember your dream of the Grecian hill-side? Well, that used to be my favourite day-dream when I was a child. Fawn-skin and all.'

To her surprise this did not elicit the reaction she had expected; she looked round at Hugh, and saw that there was a curious tense immobility about him. She waited.

Presently he spoke:

'Do you know what struck me about you when I saw you when I was Ambrosius?'

'No?'

'That you were the succuba that had haunted my dreams all my life.'

Silence fell between them again as each tried to realize the significance of what the other had said. Mona was well acquainted with what both the old theologians and the modern psychologists have to say about the demons that haunt men's sleep. She knew all about the theory of dream mechanism and wish fulfilment, and all the rest of the psychological bag of tricks. Whether there was between herself and Hugh a bond of the soul forged in ancient Greece in a bygone life, or whether she was a type that appealed to that particular sex-starved male, depended entirely upon whether one considered time as a mode of consciousness or a matter of clocks.

One thing stood out quite clearly, however, she was the solution of Hugh's problem. If she were unwilling to solve it for him, it would go unsolved. And looking deeply into her own soul she had to face the fact that although Hugh might make no appeal to her as a man, there was a queer kind of fascination about Ambrosius.

She had always had a very strong feeling for the glory that was Greece and was firmly convinced that she had been an initiate of the Mysteries of the Earth Mother. Her childish fantasy of the swift free running in the short slit kirtle that earned the Spartan girls the opprobrious title of Thigh-showers from the rest of Greece, had given place, as she grew older, to a fantasy in which she was a priestess and an initiate, penetrating deep and secret things, and the boy-comrade of the childish day-dream became the priest-initiator of the Mysteries. Not very long before Hugh had appeared on the scene, she had been reading in one of the books borrowed from Jelkes' miscellaneous stock in trade of the interpretation put by modern scholarship upon the scurrilous abuse which the Early Fathers heaped upon the pagan faiths they sought to supplant. She knew that the alleged temple orgies were far from being the *Mi-Carême* they were supposed to be, but were solemn and sacrificial acts into which no human feeling entered.

At the climax of the Mysteries of the Earth Mother all the lights went out, and the high priest and the chief priestess descended in darkness into the crypt and there consummated a union that was a sacrament just as much as eating the Body and drinking the Blood. She knew the curious magical bond that the act of union makes between a man and a woman, whether they love, or whether they hate, or whether they buy and sell in sordid indifference. If such a bond is forged by a simple animal function, what must be the bond that is forged by such a sacramental rite as that of the pastos of Eleusis?

'Do you know what I think, Hugh?' she said, breaking the long silence that had settled upon the darkening room. 'I think that there is a path opening before us, if we have the nerve to take it, that will lead us to some very wonderful things. I'll face it if you will, but remember, once we start on it, there will be no turning back.'

'That's what I have begun to suspect,' said Hugh. 'I tried

137

to turn back this morning when I got the wind up over you and Ambrosius.'

'I'll have to tackle Ambrosius and come to terms with him,' said Mona. 'It's the only thing to be done.'

'I don't envy you the job,' said Hugh. 'Personally, I think Ambrosius is quite capable of strangling you.'

'I'm not worrying about that.' Mona laid her hand on his knee. 'Do you know that there's a bond that binds me to you, just as there's one that binds you to me?'

'Yes, I know there is. I've watched you straining at it.'

'I may have done at first, but I feel differently about it now.'

'I suppose you wouldn't care to marry me, Mona?'

'Not as things are at present. It wouldn't be fair.'

'Well, I don't blame you.'

'No, I don't mean it like that. I mean I wouldn't care to take advantage of you when you aren't yourself. If I didn't really like you, Hugh, I might; it's naturally a temptation to any one placed as I am, but I'm not going to do it. If I marry you at all, I'll marry you properly, because I really want to.'

CHAPTER EIGHT

Hugh was so late getting down next morning that he had to eat his breakfast by himself, which he hated.

He could hear Mona's voice in the back premises talking to Silly Lizzie, who appeared to be in a great state of mind. There were occasional interpolations from Bill Pascoe. There did not seem to be exactly a row going on, but things sounded rather crucial. Gradually it dawned on the listener that the invocation of Pan on which they were engaged had not been without results. Lizzie appeared to think, however, that she had fallen into sin. Hugh was immensely amused at Mona's matter of fact, man-of-the-world attitude in the matter. The reprobate Bill and she were entirely of one mind and seemed to understand each other perfectly and be supporting each other warmly. Lizzie's attitude, on the other hand, was strictly conventional, and she overflowed into a squelching repentance and misery by way of compensating for her previous actions. She was also terrified of Bill's mother.

Finally Lizzie's blubbering became less stormy, and Bill's jocular basso more in evidence, and presently Mona left the happy pair to their own devices, and came out to join Hugh where he stood leaning against the door-post, smoking in the sunshine. Together they strolled slowly to the seat in the angle of the wall. Hugh gave Mona a cigarette and lit it for her.

'Mona, is this the result of the invocation of Pan I did in the chapel yesterday?'

'Yes, I expect so.'

'If it affects Silly and Bill like this, what is it going to do to us?'

Mona did not answer.

'I admit we have got better headpieces than they have,' Hugh went on, 'but it has got to be considered.'

Mona scraped the gravel with the toe of her shoe.

'What are you driving at, Hugh?'

'I think that if Pan comes through in force, he will clear out all the stopped-up inhibitions in me, and I shall be all right after that.'

She did not answer.

Hugh spoke again. 'Do you remember Des Esseintes' stunt – in Hysmans' *A Rebours*, you know? The all-black dinner-party when he wished to feel particularly wicked? Well, what about it? Don't you think we ought to be getting on with the job?'

Mona flushed at the sudden recall to the business relationship, which had gone from her mind as completely as if it had never existed.

'Yes, certainly,' she said. 'What would you like me to start on first?'

'Well, I don't quite know. I'll have to ask your Uncle Jelkes. He's the expert. But there's one thing I wish you would fit me up with, so as I can make a start, and that's a monk's robe like Ambrosius was wearing in the picture in the psalter.'

Mona raised startled eyes to his. 'What are you going to do?' she demanded anxiously.

He put his hand over hers. 'Mona, I'm going to bring Ambrosius back in good earnest. You needn't look so scared.'

He drove Mona into the little country town, and waited in the parked car in the market-place. The back view of Mona, as she stalked through the market-day crowds at her unhurried pace, recalled his dream, and something inside him stirred like a quickening child.

The draper, of whom Mona bought half a dozen yards of the coarse black serge affected by country people in mourning, wondered who the poor young lady had lost. The saddler of whom she bought a length of the white cotton rope that is used to halter beasts at shows, wondered what she was exhibiting. The shoe-maker of whom she bought a pair of sandals such as are worn by healthy lifers thought she must have a hefty pair of feet for her size.

Mona spent the afternoon in her bedroom making the coarse black serge into a cowled robe. Where or how Hugh spent it, she did not know, save that he came in to supper looking exhausted.

'I want a fitting,' said Mona in her abrupt way as soon as tea was finished.

'Right-o,' said Hugh, and followed her upstairs when she went to fetch her handiwork.

He pulled on the voluminous garment over his head like a shirt, tied the white halter-cord round his waist, and Mona knelt down at his feet to adjust the hem. He looked over her head into the mirror on the door of the wardrobe.

It gave him a very odd feeling to see himself in the long black robe with its white girdle and loose cowl around the neck. Raising his hands, he drew the cowl over his head and studied the effect of his own face, dimly seen in its shadow. He had never felt so at home in anything in his life. The long loose folds gave dignity to his lanky height. His round-shouldered stoop was appropriate in a churchman. The shadow of the cowl gave his hollow-cheeked, sharp-featured face a look of fine-drawn asceticism. He was an utterly different man.

And with the change came a sudden feeling of something dynamic; of a self-confidence and self-will he had never known before. He looked down at Mona's black head as she knelt at his feet, and prompted by some sudden mischief, he laid his hand on it.

'Pax vobiscum, my daughter,' he said.

Mona looked up, startled.

'It's all right, it's all right,' he said, patting her on the head, seeing that he had really frightened her. 'I'm not Ambrosius. I was only teasing you.'

But she continued to crouch at his feet, clutching a fold of his robe. 'You're not the Hugh I know,' she said.

He sat down on the edge of her low divan bed and drew her towards him till she was leaning against his knee. She stared up into his face, fascinated, oblivious of her position.

'What do you mean, Mona?'

'There was a rush of power through you. I don't know what it means.'

The realization came to Hugh that Mona was completely dominated by him at that moment, and he could do anything he liked with her. The feeling gave him an extraordinary exhilaration and sense of freedom and power. He felt that he must say something, anything, to assert his new dominion and make it lock home.

'This is the Ambrosius that won't take no for an answer.'

'This is the Ambrosius who won't *get* no for an answer!' and Mona suddenly smiled at him in a way she had never done before.

Hugh sat motionless, not daring to break the spell; wondering how long it would last before it faded into the light of common day.

'Do you know what I am going to do as soon as my robe is ready?' he said at length. 'I am going into the chapel, and I'm going to try and reconstruct the whole thing.'

'Aren't I coming?' said Mona.

'No,' said Hugh, 'you aren't. I'm taking no chances on Ambrosius. If I were you I'd lock your door.'

'But Hugh, you won't solve the problem with Ambrosius. It goes back further than him. It goes back to Greece – on the hill-side. And I want to be there. I'm sure I ought to be there. I'm part of it.'

'You're no part of Ambrosius, Mona. You were simply his bad dream.'

'That was his trouble, Hugh. That was what was the matter with him. It was because I wasn't there that things went wrong. They'll go wrong again if I'm not there this time.'

Hugh laid his hand on her head. 'We aren't having any human sacrifices in this temple. I'll tackle Ambrosius by myself, and then if anything goes wrong, the results will be minimal.'

Mona clutched his wrist and looked up at him with anguished eyes. 'Hugh, if I'm not there to act as lightning-conductor, it will be as if you were struck by lightning. I know it will. I felt it on a small scale just now. If I hadn't been touching you when it happened, you'd have gone right off into Ambrosius.'

Hugh leant forward and took her by the shoulders. 'Mona, that is exactly what I have got to do. I've got to go right off into Ambrosius, and then I've got to bring Ambrosius back into me.'

Mona, looking up at his face, hawk-featured in the shadow of the cowl, knew instinctively that his mental attitude was that of a man accustomed to being obeyed, like Ambrosius, who had commanded a monastery as big as a small town, not like Hugh Paston, used to being chivied by his womenfolk.

Mona kept herself busy in the garden during the days that followed. The thing she was doing was a severe strain, and it was telling on her. It was one thing to stand by Hugh with Jelkes beside her; it was another to go on day after day alone, knowing that he was experimenting all the time, and that Ambrosius was drawing steadily nearer. She was determined not to summon Jelkes because she feared that his little business might tie itself into a knot if he were not there to attend to it.

She worked steadily at the long border leading out into the field. The grey, aromatic plants were going in one by one, and the sweet sharp scent given off by their foliage as she handled them filled the air as she worked. She concentrated on her planting, knowing that from the contact she was making with the newly-turned earth she was drawing strength and stability. The great Earth-mother, feeling herself tended and served, responded.

A shadow fell across the moist, sun-warmed soil, and Mona looked up to find Hugh Paston striding past her towards the farmhouse. Mona knew instinctively that the thing she greatly feared had now arrived. Unable to concentrate on the gardening any longer, she sat down on a pile of turf and lit a cigarette with fingers that trembled.

She was not troubled about the outcome of the affair for herself; she had little or nothing to lose; it was Hugh she feared for. Would the Pan in Hugh be strong enough to break through his inhibitions? And if it did, would his nature stand the strain, or would it split?

She sat on in the sun, smoking her cigarette down to the bitter end and burning her lips before she threw it away. She was a courageous creature, and could have steered steadily through the breakers ahead had she had any sort of a chart or compasses. It was the absence of any sea-mark by which she could lay her course that gave her anxiety. She knew the general direction, but she did not know where the water might be expected to shoal and the channel would have to be kept accurately.

But there are many worse sea-marks than a star. She found herself picturing the sea of her metaphor, indigo in the darkness, flecked here and there with foam where it broke on the unseen rocks. Above her head was the night sky and the stars. The sunlight faded out, and Mona was alone with her vision. She could feel the boat of the soul that carried herself and another reaching steadily on its tack; then she put it about, and it paid off on the next long slant of the wind. The night was closing in, the wind freshening, and she thought of the Master Who had walked the waves in the storm. His comforting touch was not for her if she were following after the Wild Goat of the mountains. And then there came to her the vision of Pan with his crook, Pan as the Shepherd; Pan with his pipes – the Nether Apollo – the harmonizer. She saw him, shaggy and wild and kind, leading the creatures of the flock of Ishmael down to the grey and barren shore that lay ahead. And he held out his crook towards her over the dark waters, and she laid the course that would bring her to him where he waited, the creatures of the flock of Ishmael about his feet – creatures for whom there was no place in the world of towns and men. Somehow she knew that steering by that uplifted crook, she would come steadily through the churning white water that marked the unseen rocks.

She held on her course fearlessly, even though she could hear the breakers closing in all round her. Then it seemed to her that the Shepherd of Goats rose up gigantic in the darkness, towering above her small boat, his slanting agate eyes gleaming and kindly. He was the keeper of all wild and hunted souls for which no place could be found in a man-made world, and she and Hugh were running in under the shadow of his crook. They were coming down on to the fundamental realities of life which cannot be shaken, to which all things must come in the end. She began to feel safe and secure. Keeping her eyes fixed on the fundamental real-ity, let it be what it might, she felt certain that she would steer the right course. This was the real invocation of Pan - the surrender to bed-rock natural fact, the return to Nature, the sinking back into the cosmic life after all the struggle to rise above it into an unnatural humanity. Animal is our beginning, and animal our end, and man is a centaur who is related to Pegasus.

Mona awoke from her dream of goats and centaurs and breaking seas to find that the sun had gone in and the wind of spring was cold. The gong summoned her to lunch, but Hugh did not appear. She sent Silly Lizzie, now radiant – so radiant that Mona could only conclude that she had sinned again – up to his bedroom to see if he were there, but drew blank. Alarmed, Mona ran across to the chapel, and drew blank once more. Hurrying back through the cloisters, she noticed that the door into the main building stood ajar with the huge key in the lock. She ran from the one big room to the other, but they were empty; peered into the cellar, but that was empty too, so far as she could see; then upstairs, and along the long line of cells – all empty; up again, to the chapel in the gable – empty also. Mona, now thoroughly scared, for there was a sense of impending evil about the place, ran down the worn twisting steps of the stairs again, and down into the cellar, the only place she had not searched thoroughly. One of the cells had a door to it, and the door was closed; Mona pushed it open and looked in.

A single point of dim blue flame flickered in the darkness, giving practically no illumination; but by the light coming down the stairway behind her she saw that Hugh, clad in his monk's robe, lay on a roughly-made bench, his cowl drawn over his face. The dim blue flame came from his cigarette-lighter, which he had stood burning in a niche high up in the wall. He did not stir at the sound of the opening door. Mona, terrified, pushed back the cowl from his face, and his eyes opened and looked up at her.

'This was how it should have been,' he said, without moving.

Then Mona knew that he had been deliberately living over again his life and death as Ambrosius in the hope of picking up the lost threads of memory. The atmosphere of doom was all about him, and it was this that she had felt as impending evil and danger. Powerfully and definitely, as only a trained mind could do it, he had created that atmosphere by his picturing, and she, being sensitive, had felt it.

'This was how it should have been,' he had said. This was how the monk Ambrosius, meeting death in his sins, had pictured it. The succuba of his dreams, the woman he had never seen in real life, had come to open the prison doors, and he would be free on the hill-side of Greece where the Shepherd of Goats awaited him.

Mona took upon herself the personality of the dream-woman, the succuba, the visitant from the wide free world of the Unseen. She put out her hand and took his, knowing by the heat of his hand in hers how cold hers must feel to him.

'Come,' she said, and he rose.

He followed her up the cellar steps, cowl over face, hands in sleeves, but at the top he turned aside from the door.

'I must call them also,' he said, and went on up the winding stairs. She followed him, standing with her head just above the topmost step to watch what would happen.

He passed down the long line of the empty cells, some doorless, some with rotting doors hanging on broken hinges. Door by door, Hugh paused and called a name. Benedick, Johannes, Gyles – one by one he called the roster of the condemned monks, long since mouldered to dust. Mona wondered what spirits reborn felt a sudden stir of memory within them, a nostalgia for the Unseen.

At the end of the passage Hugh turned, and came back towards her again where she stood on the topmost step of the steep and winding stairs. He walked slowly, as befitted a Churchman, the slow swing of the skirted gown keeping time to his stride; his hands, thrust into the wide sleeves, rested folded on the knot of his girdle; his cowl was pulled forward over his face as monks use when meditating. He came and stood before her, and looking up from below, she saw his face clearly for the first time. In the shadows of the hood it looked dark and saturnine, indefinably different from Hugh Paston, and yet not Ambrosius.

He took Mona by the shoulders and held her at arm's length, staring down into her face, his own shadowed in the cowl. He began to speak in a low voice, as if communing with himself, heedless of his listener.

'I have seen you many times, near, very near, but never quite—.' He paused. 'This is what I have always wanted to do—' and he folded her in his arms. She stood for a while leaning against him, her face buried in the loose harsh folds of the monk's robe, stifled by them, but not caring to move.

'Look up,' he said at length, and she raised her head.

The dark hawk's face of Ambrosius, deep in its cowl, hung over hers.

'This is what is forbidden me,' he said, 'and that is why I am doing it,' and he kissed her. He was perfectly calm, but there was a kind of still intensity about him like the hush before a thunderstorm. Mona felt herself trembling.

They stood face to face, neither moving, and she, looking up at the harsh-featured face in the shadow of the cowl, had a sudden feeling that the fantasy was real, and that they were back in the days of Ambrosius, risking all for love under the shadow of the terrible hand of ecclesiastical power.

The man before her was a prince of the Church, powerful, ambitious; he was risking everything that made life living – more, he was risking life itself, to talk to her thus, for a few stolen moments.

And she, what was she risking? In the days of Ambrosius she would have been burnt at the stake. In the days of the present, she was risking a very nasty, possibly a pretty dangerous, experience, at the hands of an unbalanced man whom she was deliberately inciting. She might even be risking life itself, there in the empty building; many murders have been done by men in the state Hugh Paston was in. Pan in his most goatlike aspect might appear, and if thwarted, might strangle her.

Mona tried to keep a level head as she gazed back into Hugh's grey-green eyes that regarded her with a fixed, unwavering stare. But under the influence of those fanatical eyes she felt herself unconsciously slipping back into Ambrosius's century, and finding in the renegade monk confronting her a man more magnetic and fascinating than any she had ever known.

It must have shown in her eyes, for a strange look came into Hugh's for a moment. He gave a short laugh, thrust his hands into his wide sleeves after the manner of monks, and stepped back and away from her.

'This won't do, Mona,' he said. 'You go on back to the house and wait for me there.'

'Aren't you coming?' she asked, startled, fear rising in her at the thought of what might be afoot in the empty building with Hugh prowling like a ghost.

He shook his head. 'No, I am in the full tide of a catharsis, if you know what that is. Leave me alone. I'll be all right. Don't worry.'

Mona turned away and he shut the door. She knew she must leave him alone. What Hugh was going through might be truly cathartic – purge of the soul; but it put a severe strain on the integrity of the personality and she knew from Jelkes of things that happen in psychoanalyses that never got into the textbooks. Personalities sometimes come to pieces at such times, and the results have to be certified.

Hugh climbed up the worn and winding stone stairs till he came to the chapel in the gable. It had been scantily furnished with a Glastonbury chair, a press and a coffer. It was just such an equipment as Ambrosius might have had in his study, save that there was a rush mat to keep the feet from the cold of the stone – a luxury he was unlikely to have enjoyed. Hugh dropped into the Glastonbury chair, resting his elbows in the crutches of its arms, drew his cowl yet closer over his head.

He wanted to understand; beyond everything else he felt that this was his need. He had spent two hours in the dark cellar thinking of Ambrosius, thinking of him with an intensity that had reconstructed the whole medieval scene till he was living in it, and not only experiencing its emotions but feeling its sensations. He was startled to find how real the thing had become to him. It seemed as if there were not two lives, but two epochs of one life. Ambrosius, a misfit in the cloister, pagan at heart for all his priesthood, had seen God made manifest in Nature and rejected the ascetic doctrine. Ambrosius was no malignant devotee of a destructive Satan, after the manner of the old witch-cults; he sought life for deadness and light for the medieval gloom and narrowness of the cloister. Ambrosius had been broken because he had been born out of due season; he had been blackened and cut off as surely as fruit-blossom flowering too early. But the times had advanced now, and the whole age was reaching out in the same direction as Ambrosius. Supposing he could do as Ambrosius had done, and go back to the prime source of his inspiration, back beyond that disastrous medieval tragedy, might he not also contact the springs of life and live anew?

The essence of Ambrosius' problem had been that, placed as he was, it was exceedingly dangerous for him to break with orthodoxy and claim for his manhood the natural things that were denied to the Churchman. The essence of Hugh Paston's problem had been curiously similar. Hugh was deadly afraid of coming to grips with natural things amid all the artificiality of his life, lest in some unforeseen way he let catastrophe loose. The burnt soul dreads what seared it, even after reincarnation. Hugh could not grip the things that Ambrosius had burnt his fingers over.

But supposing he could go back beyond that, go back as Ambrosius had tried to do? He suddenly realized that, all unknown to himself, the thing had come about spontaneously, but had come about backwards. Not only was it possible by a careful 'composition of place' to evoke the appropriate Presence, but it seemed as if circumstances would produce the appropriate composition of place. This was a startling realization.

After all, what had his quest of Pan been save a hunger for the primitive and vital amid all the sophistication and devitalization of his life? And Pan was leading him back to the primitive along the path of his own evolution. Provided he had the courage to sink down through his own subconsciousness he would pass through the medieval darkness and tragedy and come out into the radiance that was Greece.

Hugh cast his mind back to that night in the cock-eyed old feather-bed in Jelkes' dilapidated establishment when he had invoked Pan and started everything off. When Hugh had asserted to himself the Divine Right of Nature, he had evoked Pan quite effectually. Each time he had renewed the assertion, Pan had answered. Each time he had doubted the natural divinity, the god had withdrawn. When he had kissed Mona because he was man and she was woman, she had yielded as if something deep within her had acknowledged the right; but when he behaved towards her like a gentleman, she had kept him at arm's length and found nothing in him that attracted her. There is a life behind the personality that uses personalities as masks. There are times when life puts off the mask and deep answers unto deep.

Hugh had a feeling that in doing what Ambrosius had always wanted to do and never managed – embrace his succuba – the force in himself that he called Ambrosius had found a channel.

He groped his way down the worn, winding stairs in the gathering dusk, and made his way through the cloisters to the dwelling-house, forgetting that he still wore the monk's robe. As he crossed the garth a fearful, dreadful yell re-echoed through the twilight, and he saw Bill going for his life down the drive with Lizzie running like a hare behind him. They had seen the famous ghost of Monks Farm! Hugh with a pang of compunction realized that he had upset all Mona's domestic arrangements. However, the Eleusinian Mysteries do not require an audience. 'Hekas, hekas, este bibeloi! Be ye far from us, O ye profane—' so perhaps it was just as well.

He could see by Mona's face as he entered the living-room how anxious she had been. She made tea for him, and he drank it with relief. It was pleasant to lie back in the deep chair with his feet on the hearth and a cup of tea beside him and a cigarette between his lips. For the moment, Greece and Ambrosius both seemed a long way off. But the gods are exacting, and he knew that if he strayed from the path at the present moment he might not easily find it again. He must not deviate from the concentration. Now he knew why Jelkes said that occultists trained so carefully in concentration.

'Mona,' he said, 'did you ever read *The Corn King and the Spring Queen*?'

'Yes.'

'What was the meaning of the rite in the ploughing-field, beyond the obvious, that is?'

'It was supposed to link up with the forces behind the earth and the sun.'

'Link up the individuals who took part in it, or the whole tribe?'

'Both, I suppose. The individuals wouldn't be able to link up the tribe unless they first linked up themselves. It was a sacrament. "An outward and visible sign of an inward and spiritual grace".'

'Funny thing,' said Hugh, 'Christians make a sacrament of taking life, and pagans make a sacrament of giving it.'

'They are probably different sides of the same coin, if the truth were known,' said Mona.

'Probably. Anyway, I think I've dealt with Ambrosius. I think I've absorbed him. You see, I have worked out what he wanted to do, and made up my mind to go and do it, and that settled Ambrosius. That's the way to lay subconscious ghosts, Mona – fulfil their last wishes.'

Mona sat silently staring into the fire, wondering what was going to develop, and whether Hugh had any idea where he was heading. At length she said,

'How do you propose to set about all this?'

'I don't altogether know. I've got to feel my way. The first thing is to carry out our original plan and equip the place à la Des Esseintes. I haven't felt able to tackle it before; I don't know why. But I can tackle it now all right, and I'd like to get a move on.'

'Do you want me to start collecting Tudor pieces for you?'

'No, I don't. I'm not after Ambrosius. I'm after the thing that was behind Ambrosius.'

'Greek stuff would look ghastly here, Hugh.'

'I know it would; but ultra-modern stuff wouldn't. It would look all right because it is primitive, and this place is primitive. You pick up the ultra-modern, stream-lined stuff, and it will go in all right. You mark my words, Mona, Pan is coming into his own again, and the sheer, hard, crude lines of modern design point to it. Don't you go and dig up any mock-gothic. You've got twelve days till Beltane, can you get through with it by then?'

'What do you want doing?'

'Complete reorganization. I suggest we turn this end of the building over to Bill and Lizzie. They ought to get married. They can't slosh about as they are indefinitely. The village will come up and tar and feather them. Oh, I forgot to tell you, they've bolted. Caught sight of me in my monk's kit and let out a hoot and fled. But I expect they'll flee back again in due course. They won't get much change out of Mrs Pascoe.'

A timid knock at the door broke in upon them, and Mona went to answer it. There stood two forlorn figures, who, as Hugh prophesied, had been driven forth ignominiously from the Green Man by its proprietress.

Bill told the sad tale while Silly sniffed. Mrs Pascoe, though she had seen quite fit to saddle Mona with Silly, was horrified at the idea of her as a daughter-in-law. Bill, who in his dim animal mind now regarded her as his mate, was infuriated by this insult, and, bidding mamma and all his prospects farewell for ever, had returned to Mona, braving the ghost.

Mona, laughing, opened the door and showed them

Hugh, the monk's robe hanging loose and ungirt from his shoulders like a dressing-gown, and told them that it was Mr Paston who had dressed up for a lark.

Guffaws and general relief was the result. But when asked to swear secrecy, Bill explained that it was too late, as they had already told the tale far and wide. Mrs Pascoe, it was true, had repudiated it as the result of drink, but everyone else had received it open-mouthed. He also informed them that he and Lizzie had been hand in hand to the parson to put up the banns.

Mona was appalled at the wreck of her reputation that now lay all over the village. However she reflected that the persons who were not kept away by the ghost would be maintained at a safe distance by the scandal, so they could be sure of the seclusion that is required for all occult matters.

Hugh unlocked the cellarette and handed Bill two bottles of beer to celebrate with, and the now happy couple retired to their own quarters.

Next day Hugh drove Mona up to town and dropped her in Oxford Street, arranging to meet her for tea at Uncle Jelkes', and then for the first time since the tragedy, went to his club.

It was a club that Trevor Wilmott had chosen for him. In its heyday it had been a notable institution, but it had fallen on hard times since the war, and an effort had been made to introduce some new blood into it. The new bloods were of the flashy businessman type – 'something in the City' trying to graduate into a man about town. The old brigade were of the type of Frida's father, the fag-end of the old *régime*, hanging on by their eyebrows to privilege and prestige, and keeping up their self-respect by means of mutual admiration. The more difficult they found it to keep up appearances themselves, the more exacting were their standards for other folk. Both parties regarded Hugh as an inoffensive non-entity belonging to the rival camp.

His appearance created something of a sensation. The general opinion was that Hugh would resign. All Trevor's friends were there, and all Frida's father's friends were there.

No one expected to see him walk into the dining-room and sit down and order lunch, looking particularly sprightly. Nobody quite knew the line to take. Condolences were obviously out of place, and congratulations not in good taste. Everybody waited to see what other people were going to do, and consequently nobody did anything. Hugh, who felt as if the tragedy belonged to an age more remote than Ambrosius, and had in fact, almost forgotten it, ate his lunch in peace.

He strolled into the smoking-room, reserved for members only. It was a huge room with a fire-place at each end. The one at the far end was sacred to the old brigade, the one near the door to the new blood. Hugh, standing with his back to the room, became aware that he was a focus of attention, and that it was not friendly attention. He suddenly experienced the novel sensation of feeling his hackles rise. Why should he be treated like dirt by either old has-beens or young pseudo-bucks? He turned and strolled slowly, hands in trouser-pockets, towards the sacred fire-place at the far end of the room. There, as ill-luck would have it, he came face to face with one of Frida's uncles. The old gentleman stared straight through him with a stony stare. So did all the other old gentlemen, his friends.

This was a surprise for Hugh. He had expected mutual embarrassment, which would be smoothed over by mutual courtesy; he had not expected to be outcasted. The devil entered into Hugh, and he deliberately thought of Ambrosius; as he did so, he observed a startled expression come over the faces of the old gentlemen who were supposed not to be looking at him. Hugh stared hard at his uncle-in-law, watching him slowly go from red to magenta. Still no one spoke.

Hugh broke the silence. 'You act as if it was I who had seduced your niece,' he said, and turned on his heel and walked off.

He went to the cloak-room to have a wash, and was still bending over the basin when he heard a voice behind him speaking his name in icy tones, and turned round to see his brother-in-law, the husband of his youngest sister.

'That was a pretty ghastly thing you did just now in the smoking-room, Hugh.'

'Was it?' said Hugh, rinsing his hands under the tap.

'What possessed you to act like that?'

'The devil, I expect. But there is nothing to be made out of certifying me. There's a power of attorney in existence.'

'You are insulting!'

'Well, if you will persist in ladling out unsolicited advice, you must not be surprised if you get sloshed on the nozzle occasionally.'

'My *dear* Hugh!'

'I'm not your dear Hugh. You hate the sight of me, and you know it.'

'Well, if you ask my opinion——'

'I didn't,' said Hugh.

'——there is only one thing for you to do, and that is to resign from the club, and then, in your own interests, to go to a nursing-home.'

'I'll resign from the club all right, it's no earthly use to me. And I'll withdraw my guarantee, too.'

'What do you mean?'

'Didn't you know I guaranteed the overdraft at the bank?'

'No, I didn't.'

'I thought you didn't. I guess I'll withdraw a few other guarantees and subscriptions while I'm at it.'

He straightened his back and flung the damp towel into the bin and looked at Robert. The same startled look came into Robert's face as had come into the faces of the old gentlemen in the smoking-room. Then he turned and walked off. Hugh felt certain he was using all his will-power to walk slowly.

Hugh scribbled his resignation on a half-sheet of paper, tossed it into the secretary's office, and set out for Marylebone.

In response to the clang of the bell the old bookseller appeared through the ragged curtain just as he done that night so short a while ago that had marked the turn of the lane in Hugh's life.

Hugh walked through into the inner room without waiting to be asked. He was much more at home here than he had ever been in his club. 'Going to give me a cup of tea, T.J.?' he said, and they indulged in desultory conversation while Jelkes fished a cup out of a pile of dirty crockery and gave it a rinse. Settled down with the pot on the hob, Hugh got to business. 'Uncle Jelkes,' he said, 'I'm going to seduce Mona.'

'So this is what comes of invoking Pan, is it?' said Jelkes quietly.

'Well, what did you expect? Pan was a whale on nymphs.'

Jelkes sighed. He shrewdly suspected that if Mona saw Hugh in his present mood, no assistance would be needed for the seduction. Pan had been evoked most effectually.

'Now look here, T.J., just remember that you are talking to a sight better priest than ever you were. I was running my own monastery before you had cut your pin-feathers, and it took a Pope to scrag me. Yes, I've absorbed Ambrosius, together with all his kick and go. I've only got to look at people and they wilt nowadays.'

Jelkes nodded. 'Yes,' he said. 'He'll give you self-confidence if he gives you nothing else. Given that, you can get a lot of things out of your subconscious that never went into it.'

'I don't mind what you call him, T.J. A rose by any name will smell as sweet. He's a dissociated complex, or a past incarnation, or anything else you fancy so long as you'll lend me a hand with him. As you said yourself, time is a mode of consciousness.'

'Very good, then,' said Jelkes. 'We'll take Ambrosius at his face value. If he isn't real now, he very soon will be. I'll do what I can for you, Hugh. The reason I wouldn't help with the job before was because I reckoned you'd just make use of Mona and then go back to your own kind.'

'You were wrong, Uncle Jelkes, I'm not that sort.'

'Well,' said Jelkes, 'you got Pan at the first go-off; whether he is subjective or objective doesn't matter. You mean business, and that is an effectual invocation. He will introduce you to every blessed thing you've got in your subconscious, and to every blessed thing in the racial memory that's behind you, and to the biological memory behind that to the morphological memory of all your organs, and the physiological memory of all your functions—' Jelkes stopped for breath.

'Of course the whole thing is simply the opening-up of the subconscious,' said Hugh, 'only there's a sight more in the subconscious than most people suspect. I'll leave the metaphysics to you, Uncle, I want to get on with the composition of place. It is my idea to equip Monks Farm with absolutely modern stuff instead of the mock-gothic, which was my original notion. How do you think Ambrosius will like it?'

'Well, laddie, he was a modernist in his day. What you want to recapture is not Ambrosius' limitations, but his spirit, just as he was trying to recapture the Greek spirit.'

'Then in that case we might as well go to the fountain-head and see what word the Greeks had for it.'

There was a clang of the shop-bell, and Jelkes dived through the curtain to deal with the customer, but returned instead with Mona. He watched the pair of them closely as they greeted each other. It seemed to him that there was a humorous twinkle in Hugh's eye, as if he had got something up his sleeve for Mona, but she herself was carefully non-committal.

'Well, what luck have you had?' said Hugh.

Mona did not reply, but began to unpack a small brown paper parcel she was carrying, and there appeared a little terracotta figure of the dancing Pan, skipping along with his pipes and glancing over his shoulder with a very come-hither look in his eye indeed.

'Huh,' said Jelkes. 'Very suitable. But I should keep him done up in brown paper for the present, if I were you.'

CHAPTER NINE

The days that followed were fascinating ones for Hugh and Mona. She took him among the craft-workers, disdaining shop-fronts and show-cases, and he realized the peculiar life conveyed to an article by the hand of a creative worker who is putting himself into it. Always, everywhere, through all the studios and workshops, Mona went looking for the creative spirit. Hugh was amazed to see how much of it was abroad.

The cold grey stone of the old buildings made a wonderful background for the modern colours. The stark line of modern design was at home with the simplicity of the ancient builders, though their simplicity was of necessity dictated by primitive tools and materials. Everything was ripe for the return of Pan.

The nuptials of Bill and Lizzie were due for celebration in the near future – officially, that is. Unofficially, of course, they had been in full blast for some time. The problem of housing had to be considered. Bill and Lizzie, in their dunder-headed, shuffle-footed, faithful, easy-going fashion, suited the Monks Farm *ménage* uncommonly well. The obvious thing was for the newly-married couple to move into the farm-house end of Monks Farm, and for Mona and Hugh to move out into the main building and settle down as they meant to go on.

Jelkes had given Mona a straight talking-to, but as he expected, she had declined to be sensible. 'Do you mean to marry Hugh or not?'

'Not at the moment, Uncle.'

'Why not?'

'Difficult to say. I like Hugh very much. In fact, I might say I am very fond of him; but I wouldn't worry if I never saw him again. It doesn't do to marry a man on those terms, does it?'

'Lots of women have made happy marriages on much less raw material.'

'Maybe, but not folk like me, who's been a cat on the tiles. You see, Uncle, if Hugh didn't give me all I needed in marriage, I'd find it very difficult to stick to him. I've not got the makings of a Penelope in me. It is no good promising what I can't perform.'

'You could make him a good wife if you made up your mind to it.'

'Oh no, I couldn't. I am not the stuff of which good wives are made. I'd be a top-hole mistress to the right kind of man, but I'd be a domestic fiend to the wrong one.'

'Mona, my dear, how can you say such things!'

'What a pity it is, Uncle,' said Mona, looking at him meditatively, 'that you suffer so much from repression and all your occult knowledge is wasted.'

'You are a very immoral young woman, as I've told you before,' Jelkes said.

'On the contrary,' said Mona. 'I am exceedingly moral. If I were what you say I am, I'd marry Hugh, and clear out on the alimony.'

The Eve of Beltane drew near; the moon was waxing towards the full, and everyone knew, though no one said a word, that a crisis of some sort was approaching. Finally Jelkes heaved a sigh that came from the depths of his heart, for he liked a quiet life and preferred theory to practice in occultism, packed his rush basket, locked up the shop, and took a Green Line bus.

Getting off where the lane met the by-pass, he trudged the three long uphill miles to Monks Farm, his rush basket under his arm, and arrived rather weary, for the day was close and he was not as young as he had been. However, the warmth of his welcome offset the heat of the day.

'How's the furnishing going?' asked the old man, as they sat on the bench in the angle of the wall, listening to distant church bells and bees.

'First-rate,' said Hugh. 'You wouldn't believe how well

modern stream-lined stuff fits in with Ambrosius' notion of what was appropriate in a monastic establishment. The only things that look out of place are the beds. But I'm not going to sleep on a plank bed in order to imagine I'm Ambrosius. I'm going to sleep on a decent mattress, and Ambrosius can imagine he's me.'

'I shouldn't make the drains too realistic, either, if I were you,' said Jelkes.

The sun sank red behind the fir-trees; the bees packed up and went home, and the church bells stopped ringing. Mona went in to prod the loving couple in the kitchen into activity, tactfully treading heavily as she approached the back premises.

Jelkes turned to Hugh. 'Laddie, we're tackling the job this evening.'

'What's the plan of campaign?'

'Go into the chapel, open up our subconsciouses, and see what comes.'

They parted, Hugh to the chapel, and Jelkes returning to the farmhouse. There Mona joined him.

'Where's Hugh?' she demanded possessively.

'Gone to get the chapel ready. Tonight's the night!'

'What do you propose to do?'

'Take Hugh into the chapel, build up the Ambrosius phantasy, and then psychoanalyse it.'

'And me? Do I come on in this act?'

'Yes. You will sit opposite Hugh and pick up the transference as it comes across. What you do with it after you've got it is your look-out.'

Mona answered not a word, but turned on her heel and went upstairs.

Arrived in her own room, she dragged a battered cabin-trunk into the middle of the floor, and took out a brown paper parcel, tore it open, and held up a green crêpe dress and inspected it. It was badly creased, but it would have to do. She stripped off her dingy brown jumper and skirt and slipped the clinging, flowing green over her head. It fell in long straight folds, held in place by a loose girdle with a barbaric jewelled clasp. She dived into her trunk again, and fetched out a pair of tarnished gold cocktail sandals. Mona pulled off her stockings and strapped the sandals round her bare ankles. Smoothed her thick, page-cropped hair with her brush, and bound round her sleek black head a broad swathe of the green crêpe of the dress. Then once again she dived into the ancient trunk, and brought forth a compact. By the time Mona had applied the powder and lip-stick to herself with a generous hand, the result was startling. But Mona didn't care. Something in her, that Jelkes had always known was there, had taken the bit between its teeth and was running blind.

She went downstairs to give instructions concerning supper, and was greeted with round-eyed amazement by Silly Lizzie. 'Oh, my, Miss, ain't you lovely!' Mona gave her instructions, and retreated, lest the distraction of her presence should do more harm than good.

She opened the door of the sitting-room and walked in defiantly. Jelkes looked at her amazed and raised his eyebrows. Hugh had his back to her, but at the sight of Jelkes' scandalized expression he turned round. Mona heard him gasp and saw him stiffen, and in another moment Ambrosius was in the midst of them.

The change-over was so quick that there was no moment of dazed uncertainty; so quick, in fact, that the two personalities coincided and Hugh himself was conscious of the change. For a moment the hawk-eyes in Hugh's head wavered, then they steadied and regained their calm. He stood looking down at Mona with a fixed regard. Then he turned to Jelkes.

'Now I understand something I never understood before,' he said. They both gasped, for this was Hugh, whereas they had thought it was Ambrosius.

'I understand why I went in for fast cars. It was because as soon as ever the fun began, Ambrosius took charge. Everyone always wondered how a mut like me managed it. But it wasn't me, it was me plus Ambrosius. We'll go to the chapel and tackle the job before the effect wears off.'

They made their way round the west front to the chapel, the brilliant moonlight making electric torches needless.

Hugh leading the way, robed and cowled and sandalled; Jelkes following, looking like a great moulting bird in his Inverness cape; and Mona with a dark velvety rug from the car thrown cloak-wise over her thin dress.

When they reached the chapel they saw how Hugh had spent his time. Upon the altar of the double cube that represents the universe – 'as above, so below' – stood the figure of the Piping Pan. The Glastonbury chairs formed a triangle in the sanctuary, one facing the east, and the other two facing each other. High triple candlesticks stood on either side of the altar, and in a small niche in the wall beside it was a large brass censer.

Hugh lit up the candles and switched off his electric torch, leaving their soft radiance to penetrate the gloom into the wavering shadows beyond.

Mona sat watching them, two weird figures in the uncertain light, as they wrestled with the reluctant charcoal in the censer. Then Jelkes rose upright and whirled the thing on its yard-long clashing chains round and round his head, clouds of smoke and showers of sparks flying in every direction; his enormous shadow stretched far across the vaulting of the roof, grotesque and demoniac, the cloak of his ulster flapping like the wings of a bat. Hugh, his face invisible in the shadow of his cowl, stood silently watching him. Mona clutched the arms of her chair, her heart beating in her throat and nearly suffocating her. Jelkes and Hugh, tall men in any case, looked enormous in the uncertain light. Hugh was in very deed the renegade monk returned from the tomb; Jelkes a being of another order of creation altogether.

Hugh put out his hand, and Jelkes handed the censer to him. Mona observed that Hugh handled it with the silence of an expert; there was no clashing of metal as it swung to the steady jerk of the wrist; no looping or twisting of the perverse tangle of the chains. Standing in front of the cubical altar, he censed it in due form, catching the fuming censer with a musical clash on its own chains at each return. Five swings to the left, and five to the right, instead of the orthodox three that affirms the Trinity: for five is the number of man, and ten is the number of Earth, according to the Qabalists. Ten musical clangs rang out in the shadowy darkness.

This task finished Jelkes said harshly: 'Go and sit down over there, Hugh.' Hugh did as he was bid, taking the chair facing Mona, and setting the smoking censer carefully down on the stone floor beside him. Jelkes watched the hands that remembered to arrange the trailing chains in such a manner that it could be picked up again without capsizing, and wondered what would be coming to the surface as the barriers went down.

'Now,' said Jelkes. 'Make a mental picture of Ambrosius, and look at it, and tell me what comes into your head.'

Hugh dutifully did as he was bid. They sat for a few minutes in silence. Mona could not take her eyes off the black cowled figure, sitting with bowed head intent, across on the opposite side of the sanctuary. Hugh's bare foot in its thonged sandal showed under the hem of his robe in just the same way that Ambrosius' foot had shown in the minute vignette in the psalter. Hugh she could like and pity, but Ambrosius – Ambrosius was an altogether different story.

At length Hugh raised his head and spoke.

'I think of Ambrosius going round this place keeping an eye on things while it was building, and then I think of myself doing the same thing. I think of him planning the chapel for his stunts, and I think of the kind of stunts that I'd like to have here. I think of him barging into all sorts of restrictions because he was a Churchman, and I think of myself up against things because – well, because of the way I was placed.'

'I shouldn't have thought you would have bumped into many restrictions with your resources,' said Jelkes.

'Well then, because of the way I was built,' said Hugh sulkily, and silence fell again. It is not easy to do psycho-analysis in front of a third person, especially if that person is one for whose opinion you care very deeply.

'Go on, Hugh,' said Jelkes. 'It's like a tooth-pulling, but go through with it.'

'I was just thinking,' said Hugh, 'what Ambrosius would

have done if he'd been me. For a start with, he'd have made short work of my family.'

'You seem to have made pretty short work of them yourself recently.'

'That's Mona's doing. They tried to come between her and me.' Hugh pulled up abruptly, furious at his unguarded utterance.

'What else would Ambrosius have done?' said Jelkes tactfully.

'Well,' Hugh hesitated, 'I expect he'd have got on to my wife's game early in the proceedings, and turfed her out too if she played him up the way she played me. But then she mightn't have played Ambrosius up.'

Mona gasped. That was so exactly her sentiment.

'How do you reckon he'd have disposed of her?' said Jelkes.

'Same way I did – killed her. Hadn't you realized I'd killed my wife?'

'But you didn't. She died in a motor-smash when you were miles away.'

'I bought a car for Trevor that I knew he couldn't handle. It was a kind of practical joke.'

'Did you realize what you were doing?'

'There's a little imp inside me that does things occasionally while I look the other way. If I had a row with someone I— really cared about, I could imagine myself turning pretty nasty. I could imagine myself getting my hands on to someone's throat and— and not taking no for an answer.'

'Don't you worry about that, laddie, you fetch Ambrosius along and I'll undertake to control him.'

'T.J., I'm thirty-four and you're rising seventy. Besides, you aren't here all the time.'

There was an awkward silence. Then Mona's voice came to them out of the shadows. 'I can manage Ambrosius.'

Hugh gave a short laugh that had no mirth in it.

'Yes, I bet you can – by letting him have his own way. I know Ambrosius – he is the foundation on which I am built. He's my subconscious, or part of it, anyway, and when anything happens to bring my subconscious to the surface,

Ambrosius comes up with it and takes charge. It is my solemn conviction that Ambrosius is normal, and it is Hugh Paston who is the pathology. But we can't let Ambrosius loose on polite society. I know Ambrosius if you don't.'

'I can cope with Ambrosius,' came Mona's voice again from the shadows.

'No, you can't,' said both men, hastily and simultaneously.

'Yes, I can,' said Mona. 'I'm not afraid of Pan if you are.'

'I'd never dream of letting you try to cope with Ambrosius, Mona,' said Hugh. 'He's not a man, he's a fiend.'

' "Starving men are dangerous men",' said Mona.

'And liable to turn cannibal,' added Jelkes. 'Tell me, Hugh,' he continued hastily, hoping to change the subject, 'what are the things that bring Ambrosius up with you?'

'Danger, anger, and Mona,' said Hugh curtly.

Before poor Jelkes could make another cast, Mona spoke again.

'It is my turn to be psychoanalysed now,' she said. 'And I'm going to psychoanalyse my day-dreams. They are just as useful as night-dreams if you know how to take them. When I was little I used to imagine myself racing over hills with a boy who was my brother. As we lived in the very centre of an industrial town in the Black Country and I was an only child, it isn't difficult to trace the root of that dream. When I got older and went to school I was tremendously fascinated by the Greek myths and legends. Fairy tales did not amuse me in the least; neither did stories from English history; but the Greek myths fascinated me, and I fitted my day-dream into them. Instead of running over the hills hand in hand with a brother, I was a Bacchante going out to look for Dionysus and the boy playmate was a Greek athlete who followed me because he admired me. I wore nothing but the fawn-skin because I loved to feel the sun and air.'

'That day-dream lasted a long time,' she went on. 'I put myself to sleep with it every night for years. Then, when I learnt of the Mysteries from you, I became a priestess, a pythoness, and the Greek athlete became the high priest who used me as a pythoness. That is all I remember. I have got no medieval memories, but Hugh has. Now Hugh, you take up the tale. Treat Ambrosius as a day-dream, and tell us about him.'

'Well, I think Ambrosius was a solitary, supercilious sort of being when he was a lad. Kept himself to himself and felt superior, in spite of being looked down upon locally. I think that wherever he was, he felt he didn't belong. When they put him in the Church that suited him well enough because he had got nothing to hold him outside it. Then, I think, as he got older he got it in the neck over women. Not because the old Abbot didn't ride him on a loose rein, but because he couldn't find a woman to suit him. He used to have a nightmare of a particular type of woman, and he couldn't find her in the flesh, and no one else was any use to him.'

'Have you got anything about Greece?' said Mona abruptly.

'Well now, I had as a matter of fact been constructing a Greek fantasy. I was thinking how interesting it would be to try you out as a pythoness, or priestess. I could see you walking in a procession, looking as if you came off a Greek vase. And I could see you and me up at an altar, doing a ceremony together and bringing Pan through into manifestation.'

'So your day-dreams and mine have met, Hugh?' said Mona.

'Yes,' came in a low voice from under the cowl.

'Then let's go through with it. If you will come outside, I will dance the Moon-dance for you on the grass in the moonlight,' and dropping her heavy dark wrap, she went walking down the aisle, her thin soft draperies fluttering and her golden sandals gleaming under the hem.

Jelkes hastily extinguished the candles and hurried after them.

Mona stood erect in the moonlight on the short grass of the barren pasture; the pallid light taking all colour from grass and gown and face so that she looked like a wraith. Hugh, tall and gaunt in his black cowled robe, stood a dozen yards away from her on the edge of the shadow thrown by the chapel, and even in the darkness the knuckles showed white on his clenched hands.

Then Mona began her dance. It was not so much a dance as a series of mime-gestures, for she never moved more than a few steps forward or back. A low, rhythmical humming that hardly seemed to come from human lips at all was her accompaniment, and to its rise and fall she swayed and gestured. Jelkes, knowing the symbol-language of the ancient faiths, was able to read her meaning, and wondered how much of it Hugh was picking up subconsciously. He had wanted Mona to come to an understanding with Hugh, but he had not bargained for anything quite so primitive. Mona was playing with fire, and it was a diabolical thing to do, especially with a man in Hugh's unbalanced state. Mona was a syren, drawing his very soul out of him. Hugh would never look at any other woman after this.

The dance was mime but Jelkes knew in his heart, and felt that Hugh knew also, that what was going on was very far from make-believe. Jelkes was not psychic but he could picture Mona's etheric hands going out and touching Hugh and drawing him to her, for he knew that was what she was doing in her imagination.

He pictured to himself the weaving hands drawing lines of light upon the air, and then reaching right out, like tenuous silvery tentacles, and stroking Hugh. He could see Mona's hands on Hugh's shoulders, although she was a dozen yards away. And then he saw what he had never expected to see – he saw a grey, shadowy replica of Hugh standing a yard or so in front of himself. Jelkes gasped, feeling as if the universe were turning round on him. True, he had only seen it in his mind's eye, but nevertheless, he *had* seen it, and he certainly had not formulated it. The picture had risen spontaneously without any volition on his part.

Mona had ceased her dance and was walking towards them with her normal step, no longer the curious processional pacing with which she had passed down the length of the chapel.

167

Jelkes knew at once that Mona had done as much as she meant to do for the moment, and was now pulling Hugh back to normal. But Hugh did not respond. He stood silently, looking down from his ungainly height upon Mona's face, upturned in the moonlight, his own completely hidden in the shadow of his cowl. Jelkes held his breath, wondering what was going to happen next; knowing that Mona had unleashed the wind and must now be prepared to ride the whirlwind.

Suddenly Hugh seized her by the shoulders, left bare by the loose drapery of her sleeves. Then rigid once more, he stared down at her, the expression of his own face invisible inside the cowl. Mona stood quite still, looking back at Hugh, her features clear in the bright moonlight shining over his shoulder. Her eyes were calm and steadfast, but her mouth was twitching slight.

'Where the devil are you leading me, Mona?!' he said harshly.

Hugh's grip was tightening painfully on her arms. She had a feeling that if she did not speak, did not command the situation, those hands would shift to her throat.

'Back to the beginning of things. Back to elemental nature.'

'And when we get there?'

'That I don't know; but Nature is natural, we have got to trust her.'

'I hope you know what you're doing woman!' he said fiercely. 'For there is going to be one hell of a crash if you don't.'

As he spoke, Mona felt the curious cold thrill of fear in the solar plexus that heralds the coming of the god. She caught hold of Hugh's wrists as he held her, and they stood waiting and listening. The wind was rising and rustling the thicket of overgrown laurels that flanked the chapel, and the moon, sinking to her setting, was just tipping the high gable. The weather-worn remains of the cross that had lost its arms cut the bright disk and threw its pagan shadow across them. They waited; the wind freshened; the moon slowly passed behind the gable and sank from sight.

Jelkes heard Hugh say in a low voice, 'Where is all this going to end, Mona?'

And Mona answered, 'I don't know. We have just got to trust and follow on.'

Jelkes could hardly see the two in the shadows now. Mona's drapery, grey and wraith-like, shone faintly in the dim, diffused light of the setting moon. Hugh in his black gown was invisible save for the pale blur of his face in the folds of the cowl. His two hands on Mona's shoulders alone showed up white and distinct. Jelkes expected every second to see the tense immobility of the two shadowy figures change into a desperate struggle as the forces evoked from the depths of the man's nature broke loose and took charge, and doubted whether his own strength would be sufficient to protect Mona. He opened his lips, but no words came. He tried to take a step forward, but found himself unable to move. The whole scene had changed into nightmare. Mona and Hugh were real enough; but that which lay around them was not real; another dimension had opened.

It seemed to Jelkes as if the shadows all around him were alive with forms that Hugh and Mona between them, playing with strange forces, had called to life. Was it possible that they had re-awakened the magic done by Ambrosius? Up here, at the chapel, he must have performed his rites, and things that are made with ritual live on in the memory of Nature.

This was the old magic all right, thought Jelkes, fascinated and horrified; this was what Ambrosius had been up to! That was not Hugh at all, that was Ambrosius, and he had got his hands on Mona. But what was Mona? Jelkes did not know, for that was not Mona either. It was something that was not human, something disembodied that Ambrosius had created with his magic.

All around them, and passing overhead, was the concourse of the elemental forces; powers of the air and spirits of elemental fire; souls of the waters, guardians of the treasures hidden in the veins of the earth, and all the strange familiars that served the medieval magicians. In the middle of it all stood Ambrosius with the thing he had created in his hands – the woman-form built up by his own desires; and around him were the forms of his familiars, keeping the circle secure from intrusion.

Jelkes felt the hair on his neck rising like a dog's. He was bound in the circle of that sorcery and could move neither hand nor foot, but only watch with horrified eyes what was going on before him – a renegade monk caressing the woman-form he had made by forbidden arts.

Then slowly the sight faded; the buildings and the starlight reappeared. Hugh stepped back from Mona. No one spoke. Hugh looked half-stunned. Mona seemed paralysed. Jelkes felt as if he were coming round from an anaesthetic.

Hugh raised his hands uncertainly and pushed back his cowl; Mona drew a deep gasping breath and the rigidity of her attitude relaxed. Jelkes called up all his willpower and broke through the spell. He walked up to them, put a hand on the shoulder of each and turned them about.

'Come along,' he said. 'We're going in. We've had enough of this.'

They walked beside him without word spoken; his hands on their shoulders guiding them as if they were sleep-walkers.

Back in the stuffy warmth of the living-room, Jelkes turned up the lamp as high as it would go and threw an armful of kindling on the fire. Hugh stared dazedly at the flame of the lamp and rubbed his eyes; then he dived in among the folds of his draperies and got a handkerchief out of his trouser pocket and wiped his face, which was dripping with sweat as if he had dipped it in a basin of water. He looked round at Mona, who looked back at him with non-committal eyes. She had better control of herself than either of the two men, and was like the core of calm at the heart of a cyclone.

Slowly Hugh ungirt his robe, rolled it into a bundle, and threw it into a corner of the sofa. Then he mopped his neck.

'Mona will make us some tea,' said Jelkes firmly.

Mona, only too thankful to make her escape, disappeared in the direction of the kitchen. Jelkes turned to Hugh.

'Well, what happened?' he demanded.

'God only knows! It was like a dream. I never meant to let things go as far as this. This is what I have been scared of all along. This mustn't happen again, Jelkes, it isn't fair to anybody.'

Mona entered with a tray of crockery. She did not look at them, and they did not look at her.

'What are we going to do about it?' asked Hugh as she went out again.

'I'll speak to her,' said Jelkes.

'Somebody certainly ought to. I don't think she knows what she's about.'

Mona came in again, a big brown earthenware bowl between her two hands. She paused in the doorway and stood looking at them. Still in her green dress and with the fillet about her hair, she looked, as Hugh had said, like something off a Greek vase. Hugh was staring at her fascinated, oblivious of all else. She stood looking down at Hugh as he half sat, half crouched in the deep chair. Her face was calm. Her eyes were steady, but the usual close-held line of her mouth was relaxed, and her lips were full and very scarlet and in the hollow of her neck a pulse was beating visibly. Jelkes came to the conclusion that Mona knew exactly what she was doing, and that it was not the slightest use to speak to her.

The meal was eaten in silence, save for the necessities of the table. Jelkes and Mona drank the everlasting tea, and Hugh, though he forewent spirits out of deference to Jelkes, felt he owed himself something, and opened a bottle of beer.

The party broke up and went to their rooms as soon as the meal was over. Jelkes wondered whether it was his duty to patrol the passages, but concluded that it was better to leave things to nature and pulled the bedclothes over his head with a profound sigh. What would be, would be, *Dei et Diaboli volunti.*

Mona sat up in bed, her arms tight folded round her knees to prevent them from shaking, and asked herself what in the world had possessed her to act as she had. Not having the kind of conscience that prevaricates with herself, Mona did not deny that Ambrosius, the renegade monk, had a diabolical fascination for her; but to stir up the Ambrosius aspect of Hugh was to play with fire. Ambrosius was Hugh's repressed subconscious, built up into a secondary personality. If she played the fool with him any more, he might have a nasty breakdown, and even come within genuine reach of certification. She blamed herself bitterly. Why had she let herself get carried away like this? She knew, too, that Jelkes was angry with her, and that vexed her still more, for she had a very great respect for him, and valued his good opinion highly.

She felt certain that Jelkes hated Pan, if the truth were known, and was perpetually making the Sign of the Cross inside himself, thus preventing Pan from manifesting and so throwing everything into confusion. Mona flung angrily away from all restraints, and yet her self-respect prevented her from yielding to Pan in his satyric aspect. The world was too much for her, and she longed for the vales of Arcady.

Hugh, on his side, stood with his hands in his dressing-gown pockets staring out of the window at the starlight. He had had a pretty thorough shake-up, and sleep was far from him. He knew with a sense of delighted triumph that Mona had let herself go far more than she had ever meant to; but he had also sensed the reaction that had been coming on steadily all through supper. He was quite alive to the fact that it was Mona's fixed intention not to involve herself with him. He, for his part, felt that everything life held for him was bound up with Mona. His negative, hypersensitive nature clung to Mona's dynamism as the one thing that would enable it to go on living in a world that had been all darkness and coldness. He had come to the point when he was beginning to feel pretty desperate; if Mona wouldn't have him, he didn't know what he was going to do.

It seemed to Hugh that surely out of all her richness and abundance the Great Mother could meet his need? Why forget the Mother in the worship of the Father? Are the descending Paraclete and the uprising Pan two opposing forces locked in an everlasting struggle, or are they an alternating current playing between the two poles of spirit and matter?

Hugh did not know. Metaphysics had never been his strong point. He knew what his need was, and he considered it to be a legitimate need, and he did not see why he should be expected to deny it fulfilment.

Why had Mona never mated during her thirty-odd years? What was she asking of men that they did not give her? Were there no priest-initiates now to work with her the rites of Eleusis? Perhaps that was the trouble. And he debated whether it was feasible for him, Hugh Paston, to assume the part of the priest of the Mysteries. Could he, by imagining himself to be the Greek priest-initiate, identify himself with Pan?

He and Mona were not boy and girl on the hills in the sun, but mature man and woman, who asked more of mating than would have satisfied the Greek athlete and his lass. They were priest and priestess. In Mona's phantasy the priest had been the initiator who had admitted her to the Mysteries. If he played the part of the high-priest he would soon feel sacerdotal: especially if he could inveigle Mona into playing the part of the pythoness.

Lost in his day-dream, Hugh stood on, oblivious of the passage of time. The bare grey stone of the English building gave place to the white marble of a Greek temple; the pale starlight of an English night to flickering Greek torches. He was the high-priest in the sanctuary awaiting the coming of the priestess. Beyond the curtains, Tyrian-dyed, he could hear the murmur of the crowded, excited temple. The curtains parted, and Mona stood before him in her robe as priestess of Ceres, the curtains falling again immediately behind her. The crowded temple hushed and held its breath. This was the sacrament, the bringing through of power. This was the sacerdotal office. Behind him was the All-Father, the First-Begotten Love, behind her was the Earth-Mother. As in the phantasy, he had become the priest, now the priest became the god – spontaneously, without any volition on his part. He felt power come upon him, he felt himself part of a larger whole, made one with the earth as she swung through the circling heavens. And then he checked and stayed. He could go no further. He lacked his priestess. The power that had sought expression through him could find no passage, for the circuit did not lead to earth but remained insulated in empty space. The reaction hit him hard. He knew that he had been within an ace of the thing he sought, and the missing of it gave him a sense of irritated frustration that promised badly for his nerves next day.

His mind turned back to Arcady. There, and there alone, lay the fulfilment of both promise and dream. The Arcadian Pan with his shepherd's pipe was no diabolical deity, like the sinister Goat of Mendes of the inflamed medieval imagination. It was the thing behind Ambrosius he must go after – the Greek inspiration that had awakened Ambrosius to his manhood. Hugh wondered whether his own problems were not part of a universal problem, and his own awakening part of a much wider awakening? He wondered how far the realization of an idea by one man, even if he spoke no word, might not inject that idea into the group-mind of the race and set it working like a ferment?

Supposing, thought Hugh, absorbed and completely oblivious of his surroundings – supposing he were to phantasy the part of the Greek high-priest of Mona's day-dream until it became alive in him even as Ambrosius had done, might not Mona answer to it? Hugh remembered Mona's words in the chapel concerning the Greek athlete of her phantasy who had followed her because he admired her. That, of course, was his own dream precisely. He remembered the tense look on Mona's face when he had casually told that dream as they were looking at the dusty old books in the museum. She had recognized it all right, and for some reason best known to herself had made open confession when they were psychoanalysing themselves in the chapel. Was there something in Mona that was saying, 'Yes, I will worship Pan with you provided you are of the true faith'?

It seemed to him that if he could pull this thing off with Mona something would be brought through into the group-mind of the race and added to the racial heritage – that, at any rate, was the way Jelkes said the adepts worked.

There came to him, as he stared at the marvel of the night-sky, a realization that he was part of a larger whole and that a vast life found expression through him, and that in his fulfilment it would find a measure of its fulfilment, and in his frustration it was frustrated. It was not a question of Hugh Paston being in love with a woman who did not respond to him, it was a question of unbalanced force in the universe, and he knew that the whole universe was striving to adjust that unbalance, and that if he would but lean back and let himself be borne by the cosmic tides, they would bring him to the place where he would be.

He felt that he had stumbled on a very important key when he had realized that the way of approach to the dynamic reality lay by the path of phantasy, the most dynamic of all auto-suggestions. It might be pure imagination, but nevertheless it was the way to set the invisible causes in motion, provided it lay along the line of their course.

This was indeed a discovery worth making. He had only to become the priest and he could command his priestess.

CHAPTER TEN

The sun rose next day through the morning mists with a promise of heat, one of those brief miniature heatwaves that sometimes come in the days between spring and summer, and Hugh, feeling the breathing warmth coming in at his open window as he dressed, felt a strong disinclination for heavy stuffs and stiff collars, and clad himself in an old pair of khaki shorts left over from his African expedition, a short-sleeved khaki mesh shirt minus most of its buttons, and Ambrosius' sandals. In this disreputable kit he descended to breakfast.

He moved silently in the heelless sandals, and came into the living-room without Mona being aware of his presence. As upon the day of their first morning meal at the farm, the door leading out to the garden was wide open to admit the morning sun and the table stood before it, a small oak gate-legged table covered with a gaily-coloured, coarse-textured, hand-woven cloth on which stood the hand-thrown earthenware breakfast set, all yellow and orange on the greyish-buff ground of the natural clay. As before, the brown velvety faces of polyanthuses rose from their little honey-pot, but whereas on that day they had been the first bold venturers from under a sunny wall, these were the last lingering laggards from a shady corner. Mona, singing softly to herself, was rearranging the haphazard efforts of Silly Lizzie in the way of table decoration, and the song she sang was a curious one.

> 'Bowl of oak and earthen jar,
> Honey of the honey-bee;
> Milk of kine and Grecian wine,
> Golden corn from neighbouring lea –
> These our offerings, Pan, to thee,
> Goat-foot god of Arcady.

'Horned head and cloven hoof –
Fawns who seek and nymphs that flee –
Piping clear that draweth near
Through the vales of Arcady –
These the gifts we have of thee,
God of joyous ecstasy.

'Come, great Pan, and bless us all:
Bless the corn and honey-bee.
Bless the kine and bless the vine,
Bless the vales of Arcady.
Bless the nymphs that laugh and flee,
God of all fertility.'

It was oddly appropriate to the simple breakfast-table set there in the sun, from which only the Grecian wine was lacking, and Mona, who, like Hugh, had felt the early heat and put on her thin green frock, was the appropriate priestess. She had her old brown sandals on her stockingless feet, and there was no fillet on her hair, but save for that, she was exactly as she had been the previous evening when she had danced the moon-dance for the drawing-out of Hugh's soul.

She looked up and saw him there and stood clutching the little bowl of flowers in her hands helplessly. Sleep and the sunshine had enabled her to put her problems behind her for the moment and escape into the vales of Arcady. She had not expected Hugh to be down just yet, and, taken by surprise, could find no word to say save: 'Hello.'

'Hello, Mona,' he replied.

She tried desperately to discern from his bearing what his interpretation might be of the previous evening's happenings. But there were times when Hugh was as impassive as an effigy on a tomb.

'Isn't it a lovely morning?' she said nervously.

'Very lovely. I think' – a smile appeared at the corner of his mouth – 'that Pan must be pleased with us.'

Then, to Mona's intense relief, Jelkes joined them clad in the everlasting Inverness, despite the warmth, and they sat down to the milk and the honey and the porridge and the new-laid eggs and whole-meal bread in the sunshine – a truly Arcadian meal.

Mona departed to the back premises to start Silly Lizzie off with a push; Jelkes sat himself down in the sun with a sensational Sunday paper and proceeded to soak his soul in scandal, and Hugh wandered off across the pasture smoking his after-breakfast cigarette.

He had an instinctive feeling that the chapel was not a suitable place for the invocation of Pan – he doubted if any roofed place ever could be. The great archangels in the buttress bays were the austere regents of the elemental forces and the mystical Tree in the east had meanings to meditate upon for a lifetime, but Pan was another matter. It was in Hugh's mind that a coffer, up-ended, would serve as a cubical altar, and it was in his mind to shift it out into the pine-wood if he could find a place unobserved from both the house and the road.

He strolled slowly down the broad grassy way between Mona's newly-planted herb-beds, plucking here and there grey aromatic leaves, crushing them in his hands, and inhaling their clean, sharp odour from between his cupped palms.

They had never explored the wood very thoroughly because it was beset with brambles, but Hugh, taking giant's strides, lifted his long bare legs over these and reached its shade, hoping to find some sort of cover among the undergrowth.

He pushed on, finding it easier going now that the shade made all growth scanty and saw ahead of him a dense mass of dark foliage among red-brown trunks. He headed towards it, to find a close-set belt of yews blocking his path. The yew is a long-lived, slow-growing tree, and from the girth of these he judged they must be pretty ancient, and with a sudden quickening of heart-beat, wondered whether they dated from Ambrosius' day, and if so, why they had been planted?

He ducked under the low-hanging outer branches, and with some difficulty forced his way through, to come out into a little open glade entirely surrounded by yews. Here was the very privacy he desired!

All round him the green-black branches of the yews swept the very ground in a long narrow oval. The glade was the exact shape of the space made by two intersecting circles, and had evidently been laid out with mathematical precision. In the exact centre of the rabbit-nibbled turf an oblong boulder reclined upon its side. Hugh examined it. It was difficult to tell, so weather-worn it was, whether it was a natural outcrop or a tooled stone. The chalk, however, does not produce such stones as this, and Hugh, looking at the long narrow rock at his feet, guessed that it was one of those standing-stones of which Mona had spoken – a sighting-stone along a line of power. Ambrosius had chosen his site well. Around the ancient standing-stone he had planted his grove of yew, thus ensuring it being right in the track of one of the lines of force of the ancient worship.

Hugh considered the great stone as it lay humbled in the dust. It would not take a great deal of work to set it up again. He thought he could do it single-handed, with luck. Pushing his way through the yews, he set off at a dog-trot for the house, skirted round to the potting-shed unobserved, and returned with pick and spade. The loose sandy soil worked easily, but up-ending the great stone was another matter, and sorely against his will, Hugh had to go and fetch Bill.

Amiable as the bob-tailed sheep-dog he so closely resembled in everything save intelligence, Bill shoved through the bushes in his Sunday best in the wake of his employer. When he saw the stone, however, he pushed his peaked cap on to the back of his head and scratched it.

'Oy,' he said. 'That's one of the Devil's skittles.'

'Maybe, but we're going to up-end his stone and put it tidy for him.'

'Aye, aye, sir,' said Bill, gave the stone a mighty heave, and set it upright in the hole that Hugh had dug under its base. Together they filled in the loose earth and trod it firm.

Bill shouldered the pick and spade and ambled off, leaving Hugh to consider the next move. Having a standing-stone in the centre of the glade, he needed no other altar.

He examined it closely, and decided that it was certainly a worked stone – a short, blunt pillar with a rounded top, it was too symmetrical to be anything else.

In response to his message sent by Bill, lunch was in the open. Mona served them – it was no use getting Silly Lizzie to wait at table if you did not like your food down your neck – and they settled down to their meal. Suddenly old Jelkes looked up, and breaking his usual rule of silence while feeding said:

'I reckon you are right to go through with this thing, Hugh, and I'll do anything I can to help you, even if I do get knotted up in my own complexes sometimes. It's that monk's cowl that does for me. After all, I was very nearly one myself!'

'Hugh said a true thing once,' said Mona. 'Or maybe it wasn't Hugh but Ambrosius. I can't tell them apart these days. He said that the Church was made for man, not man for the Church.'

'I reckon that's about it,' said Jelkes. 'After all religion is simply our speculation about what lies below the horizon of life. The only way you can judge a theology, so far as I can see, is by its effect on character. You can see its effect on human life. I look at their adherents – the general run of them – not the saints – not the black sheep, but the bulk. Christianity produces too many fiends and tolerates too many fools. It's the worst persecutor of the whole bunch. Islam goes in for jehads and massacres, but there's no petty spite about it. I reckon that group-souls get neuroses, same as individuals, and that Christianity is suffering from old-maid's insanity from too much repression; that's what makes it so damned unchristian.'

'You are blaspheming abominably, Uncle,' said Mona. 'If I said the half of this, you'd screw my neck.'

'It isn't as bad as it sounds, my dear,' said Jelkes. 'It is the Church I'm slanging, not the Christ. It is function, not charter, that confers rights in religion. I defer to the man with genuine spiritual power, and I don't care a hoot in hell whether he has been ordained or not.'

Sitting on the low, broad bench, with the man and the

girl on either side of him, Jelkes stared out towards the sun that hung golden over the pine-wood.

'What is going to be the next move in the game?' he said at length.

'The next move,' said Hugh, 'is to return to our original plan, and invoke Pan by a blend of Ignatius and Huysmans. It is in my mind that we've travelled a good long way already; perhaps further than any of us realize.'

Jelkes cocked an eyebrow at him. 'What makes you think that?' he said.

Hugh pushed back his seat and rested his sinewy elbows on his great gaunt knees – he looked much bigger and more formidable thus sketchily clad than in his ordinary clothes.

'Difficult to say,' he said at length. 'One expects psychic phenomena to be reasonably tangible and to have something of the miraculous about them. We've had nothing of that. But all the same we've had – or at any rate, I've had, some pretty drastic experiences. I couldn't prove them to anybody else, but I'm quite satisfied about them in my own mind. Anyway, whatever they are, subconscious, super-conscious, hallucinations, telepathy, suggestion, auto-suggestion, I feel as if I had been born again, born into a wider life and a bigger personality.'

'How do you know it isn't all your imagination, Hugh?' asked Jelkes, watching him.

'I don't know and don't care. It probably is, for I've used my imagination diligently enough over the job. But *via* the imagination I've got extended consciousness, which I probably wouldn't have got if I'd stuck to hard facts and rejected everything I couldn't prove. It's no use doing that. You've got to take the Unseen as a working hypothesis, and then things you can't prove at the first go-off prove themselves later. By going ahead "as if", I've got in touch with another kind of reality and in that kind of reality I can pull the strings that make things happen – and damn it all, Jelkes, I'm going to!'

'It appears to me,' said Jelkes, 'that if Mona is to remain here alone with you, she would be well advised to lock her door.'

'That's what I told her,' said Hugh. 'But she doesn't do it.'

'How do you know I don't?' cried Mona indignantly.

'Because I took the key away some time ago, and you've never missed it.'

Mona sprang to her feet with the heavy earthenware pitcher in her hand.

'If you throw that water over me, you'll get what's coming to you,' said Hugh.

Jelkes got on to his feet and pounded the table like a chairman at a disorderly meeting. 'You'd better marry him, Mona, and be done with it. It will save us all a lot of trouble.'

Mona, speechless with rage, poised the heavy pitcher in her hand as if about to heave it at them both simultaneously.

'It doesn't matter to me,' said Hugh airily. 'The ceremony is not of overwhelming importance in the circles in which I move.'

'Nor in the circles in which I move,' said Mona. 'But I'm damned if I'm going to be bounced in this manner.'

'Well, will you marry me or not?'

'No, blast you, I won't!'

'Oh, my Gawd!' said Jelkes, dropping down on the bench and resting his head on his hands.

Hugh patted him on the back. 'Cheer up, Uncle; we're enjoying it, even if you aren't. This is love among the moderns. Look at Mona, she's thriving on it – Hi, you little devil!' He fielded the pitcher neatly, but the water went all over Jelkes, who rose and shook himself like a wet cat, looking most indignant.

'If this is love among the moderns, give me hate,' he said. 'I don't know how you tell 'em apart,' and stalked off into the house, slamming the door behind him.

Hugh set down the pitcher out of Mona's reach.

'Well, what about it? Will you marry me?'

'*NO ! ! ! !*'

'Splendid, I'll see about the licence.'

'It will be wasted.'

'Doesn't matter if it is. If you throw that dinner-plate, I'll spank you with it.'

Mona sank down on the bench as Jelkes had done, and clutched her head.

'Oh, my God! I wouldn't have believed it of you, Hugh. I suppose I may as well. I'll get no peace till I do. But it was taking that key away that annoyed me.'

'But I didn't do it. I only said I'd done it.'

'Then you're a damned liar! Whatever possessed you to say that?'

'I wanted to see if you really had locked your door after I warned you. Because if you hadn't, it was safe to bully you into a wedding, for your subconscious had spoken for you,' and he bent down and kissed her.

Pending the three intervening weeks, while the vicar would be announcing the banns of employers and employees, Hugh bid Mona collect a suitable trousseau in which, he said, green should predominate as she was being dedicated to Pan.

Mona agreed, while doing hasty mental arithmetic, too proud to ask for a halfpenny. But when the post came in, she waved before him a printed form in speechless indignation: a considerable sum of money had been placed to her credit at her bank.

'What's the meaning of this?' she demanded, as if direly insulted.

'Well, I didn't want you to take my instructions too literally and turn out in a fig-leaf, not in this uncertain weather, anyway. I want you to do the thing properly, *à la Huysmans*.'

'Indeed?' said Mona, 'and what would you consider to be garments appropriate to Pan?'

'Well, strictly speaking, none at all, but as it's an English spring—.'

'I wish Uncle were here to tell you what he thought of you.'

'Can't you design something for yourself, same as you did for the house? I want you to feel unrepressed.'

'I *am* unrepressed!' snarled Mona, furious at this aspersion on her modernity.

'No, you aren't or you wouldn't snarl. Unrepressed people

have sweet tempers, for they are absolutely spontaneous and free from conflict.'

'If I were absolutely spontaneous and free from conflict, you'd be lying dead at the moment.'

'It is a curious thing,' said Hugh, 'that in the days when I was a decent citizen, you posed as a cat on the tiles, and now that I've taken you at your word and joined you on the tiles, you bolt for the hearth-rug.'

'All right. Anything for a quiet life. I'll do what you want, but I hate you giving me money.'

What she proposed to do he neither knew nor inquired; but he returned one afternoon from a session with Mr Watney to find the farmhouse standing empty, and felt a sudden chill feeling of hurt, for it was the first time he had ever returned to the farm and Mona had not been there to welcome him. Then a sound in the old part of the building caught his ear, and he went quickly towards it. At the foot of the beautiful spiral stair stood a woman of the Renaissance.

He halted, completely taken aback. He adored Mona, but it had never occurred to him before to consider her beautiful. She was dressed in a full-skirted, tight-bodiced robe of heavy brocade. The ground colour was fawn, faintly dusted with gold by an occasional gold thread in the warp, and peacocks and passion flowers interlaced all over it in a dazzle of green and blue. The neck of the tight-fitting bodice was cut square and low, and behind Mona's smooth dark head rose a high collar of gold.

Hugh came towards her. 'What are you doing in here?' he demanded, to cover his emotion, for the sight of her in her *cinquecento* robes affected him beyond all reason. She was a woman of Ambrosius' age!

'I am trying on my frocks against their proper background,' said Mona with dignity, but as red as a paeony. 'I had not expected you back so soon.'

'So you've chosen the Renaissance for your period?' said Hugh slowly. 'Now why that, and not Greek draperies?'

'Because I *am* Renaissance,' snapped Mona, tossing her head.

He looked at her without speaking. 'Yes,' he said at length 'I think you are.'

Thrown in a heap on a broad divan were a pile of garments; there was a rust-red robe with a bold gold pattern of dragons upon it; there was a deep, intense blue, patterned in silver like a moonlight night; these were heavy and stiff brocades, full-skirted, tight-bodiced. But there were also diaphanous stuffs that flowed like water, cloud-blue, dusk-grey and leaf-green. The whole pile was shimmering and opalescent, for the diaphanous stuffs seemed to have under-dresses of silver and gold tissues.

Mona disappeared behind the stairs, to return in a moment clad in her usual garments with her glory over her arm, gathered up the heap of opalescence, and stalked off in her usual sturdy manner across the cloister garth to the farmhouse, Hugh behind her. The glory was departed; Mona was back to her normal, but Hugh had had a glimpse of that other self in her, the Renaissance self, that lay there under all, waiting to be called into life, and he was not likely to forget.

There came a day when they all packed into the Rolls-Royce and turned up at the village church to supervise the making one of Bill and Silly. Mr and Mrs Huggins were there; they delighted in doing anything that could possibly annoy Miss Pumfrey. Mr Pinker was not there, though he turned up at the wedding breakfast and did his share and something over, explaining apologetically that he could not afford to quarrel with Miss Pumfrey and the vicar. Even Mrs Pascoe was there, to Silly Lizzie's horror, who was certain she had come to forbid the banns, and was with difficulty prevented from turning back and bolting forth-with. But Mrs Pascoe had proved a ready convert when told that Miss Pumfrey was infuriated at the idea of any orphan of hers getting married, and had threatened to invoke the power of the law to prevent such an indecency. The vicar eyed them with a sour eye and broke the speed record for the diocese. Thereafter there was a noble binge at the Green Man, and Mr Huggins had to be driven home round the common in Mr Pinker's gig because he was incapable of walking. Bill and Silly then went off for a week at Southend at Hugh's expense, and stopped on for another week at the rate-payers' expense for having been drunk and disorderly.

Thereafter Hugh and Mona were free to attend to their own affairs. They drove up to town, collected Jelkes from among his books, and as Mona's flat was just over the Marylebone boundary, set off for the registry office. Having paid this tribute to the gods of England, they both kissed the blushing Jelkes and returned to Monks Farm and the gods of Greece.

The full moon rode high and cloudless over Monks Farm. As far as Hugh and Mona's outward demeanour was concerned, this evening in no way differed from any other evening at Monks Farm, save that Lizzie was not there to do her little jobs with such painstaking care and incompetency.

Monks Farm was quiet with a quietness that seemed almost uncanny to the ears that had rung with the noise of London all day. A dog barked on a far-off farm; a misguided rooster crowed; and between each sound there were long spaces of warm scented stillness as a faint breeze stirred soundlessly in a line of ancient thorns, laden with blossom. The afterglow faded from the west, and a bright low star came out over the pines.

'Our star,' said Hugh, squeezing Mona's arm where his hand lay. 'Come along, I've got something to show you. But first we must assume our Pan wedding-garments.'

When Mona rejoined him she wore floating green, but the moonlight took all colour from it and she looked like a grey wraith. Hugh himself wore the traditional fawn-skin.

They went down between the herb borders, hoary silver in the dusk, crossed the bare pasture, and entered the pinewood, now cleared of brambles. In the dense belt of yews an arch had been cut. They came out into the little, lozenge-shaped glade bathed in moonlight, and away scurried dozens of rabbits, all except one baby thing that lost its head and took refuge in the shadow of the pillar and stayed there throughout the proceedings, as if representing its Master, the Lord of the Wild.

Hugh offered no explanation, and Mona offered no comment. Neither were needed. He placed her at one end of the enclosure, and took up his own position at the other, the new-risen moon behind them. Then he waited for inspiration, for he had no idea what a rite of Pan might be.

Silently they waited, and time went by, but it did not seem to drag. Both were thinking of the ancient rites of Eleusis, and wondering in what form the power of the god would come upon them. Once only Hugh stirred, to raise his arms in invocation. Mona never moved. The turf beneath their feet retained the heat of the day, though the air was slowly chilling with the evening damp.

Hugh's thoughts went back to his dream of the hills of Greece: perhaps there he would pick up the trail. He followed in his mind the path of the dream, up the steep hillside, through the sparse wood, and then, almost involuntarily, he entered the deeper wood and felt the cold pang of fear that lurked there waiting for him. He felt it in the solar plexus, like a hand gripping, and a shudder went all over him. He saw the hanging points of Mona's drapery flicker, and knew that she had shuddered too. Then he saw that between them was a path of pale gold light, and it was not moonlight.

A breath of wind began to stir in the narrow space between the encircling yews, a little cold breath of air that moved softly over them, as if feeling them, paused, and moved again and was gone. Then the temperature began to rise. It rose steadily, rapidly, till Hugh felt the sweat break out on his chest, left bare by the fawn-skin. He found it hard to breathe, and his breath came short and quick. The band of light across the turf rose hip-high. It bound him to Mona as the current binds a man to the live rail. It was far stronger than he expected, and again came the pang of fear.

Then the place began to fill with light, overpowering the oppressive heat. It was a curious light, neither of the sun, nor of the moon, nor of the stars; more silver than the golden band that still shone amid it; less silvery than the pale moonglow and the stars. And in this light all things were reflected. The earth spread away into space in a great curve, with their grove upon it. It swung through the heavens in a yet greater curve, the planets circling around it, and it was ringed like Saturn with luminous bands. This was the earth-aura, and within it was lived their life. Their psychic selves breathed in those bands of light as their physical selves breathed in the atmosphere. And within the earth was the earth-soul, all alive and sentient, and from it they drew their vitality.

Mona knew that these things were there all the time, though in their normal state they were unaware of them; but Hugh thought that they had come at his invocation, and felt that the whole swinging sphere circled about him, and for a brief moment knew godhead.

Then the light returned to focus on the glade, leaving behind, like a receding tide, the memory of the environing infinity, never to be effaced. For ever after Hugh would live his life against that background and measure all things by it.

The glade was softly luminous, very hot, and a band of glowing gold, like illuminated smoke, stretched from Hugh to Mona, flowing around the pillar, whose conical top rose just above it. Behind Hugh was the newly-risen moon and his face was in darkness, but Mona's showed clear in the moonlight. He could see her eyes, but she could not see his, and her look had a blankness in consequence, as if she were looking beyond him at something that stood behind. Perhaps she was: for at that moment a gradually dawning awareness made itself felt, and Hugh knew that something was behind him, vast and overshadowing, and that from it emanated the band of light that passed through him and fell upon Mona. He felt himself getting vaster and vaster, and about to burst with the force that was upon him. He was towering up, his head among the stars; below him, Mona and the earth lay in darkness. But over the earth-bend the advancing line of dawn was creeping up, then he realized that this was no earthly dawn, but the coming of the sun-god.

Yes, it was not the goat-god, crude and earthy. It was the

sun! But not the sun of the sophisticated Apollo, but an older, earlier, primordial sun, the sun of Helios the Titan. Hugh had not known what Freudian deeps they would work through in the name of the goat-god, and was prepared for anything; but this golden exaltation of high space took him completely by surprise. Then he remembered. 'All the gods are one god, and all the goddesses are one goddess, and there is one initiator.' The All-Father was celestial Zeus – and woodland Pan – and Helios the Life-giver. He was all these things, and having known Pan, a man might pass on to the heavenly gate where Helios waits beside the Dawn.

Hugh felt his feet winged with fire, and knew that he was coming as the Angel of the Annunciation came to the Virgin: he was coming as the messenger of the Life-giver. Far below him Mona waited in the earth-shadow, and it seemed to him that she was in some way lying back upon the earth and sunk in it, like a swimmer floating in water.

And he knew that he was coming swiftly on the wings of the dawn, coming up with the dawn-wind as it circled the earth. He could see the line of golden light advance, and knew that his return to the grove would coincide with its coming.

Then he found himself standing in the grove, in his own body, clad in the fawn-skin, and the line of light was just beyond his feet. For the first time since the vision began he moved, taking a step forward. The line of light advanced with him. He took another step forward; it advanced again. Mona also had taken two paces forward. He moved again, and the light and the woman moved also.

Now they were standing face to face upon either side of the pillar. Hugh raised his sinewy bare arms and stretched them over Mona's head, and the light that had enveloped him spread over her also. Then, raising his right hand in the Salute of the Sun he lowered the left, tingling and burning with a strange heat, and laid the flat palm between Mona's breasts and cried the ancient cry – 'Hekas, Hekas, este bibeloi! Be ye far from us, O ye profane.'

A MAGICAL INVOCATION OF PAN

I am She who ere the earth was formed
        Rose from the sea.
O First-begotten Love, come unto me,
And let the worlds be formed of me and thee.

Giver of vine and wine and ecstasy,
God of the garden, shepherd of the lea –
Bringer of fear, who maketh men to flee,
   I am thy priestess, answer unto me!

Lo, I receive the gifts thou bringest me –
Life, and more life, in fullest ecstasy.
I am the moon, the moon that draweth thee.
I am the waiting earth that needeth thee.
   Come unto me, Great Pan, come unto me!

(from 'The Rite of Pan')

STAR BOOKS

are available through all good booksellers but, where difficulty is encountered, titles can usually be obtained *by post* from:

Star Book Service,
G.P.O. Box 29,
Douglas,
Isle of Man,
British Isles.

Please send retail price plus 8p per copy.

Customers outside the British Isles should include 10p post/packing per copy.

Book prices are subject to alteration without notice.